MY
Invented
LIFE

LAUREN BJORKMAN

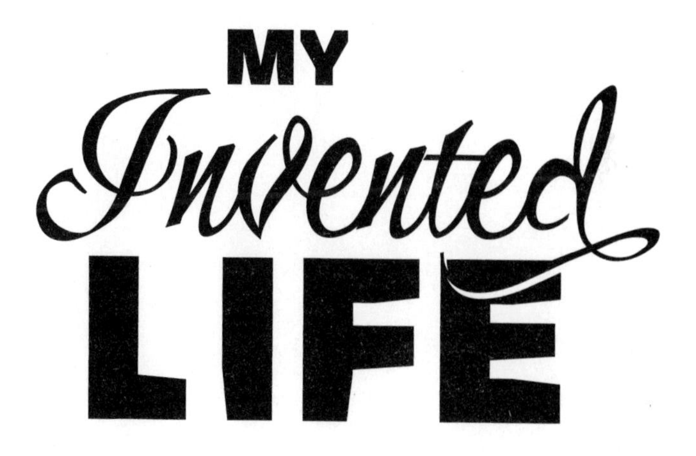

Henry Holt and Company
NEW YORK

Henry Holt and Company, LLC
Publishers since 1866
175 Fifth Avenue
New York, New York 10010
www.HenryHoltKids.com

Distributed in Canada by H. B. Fenn and Company Ltd.

Library of Congress Cataloging-in-Publication Data
Bjorkman, Lauren.
My invented life / Lauren Bjorkman.—1st ed.
p. cm.
Summary: During rehearsals for Shakespeare's "As You Like It," sixteen-year-old Roz, jealous of her cheerleader sister's acting skills and heartthrob boyfriend, invents a new identity, with unexpected results.
ISBN 978-0-8050-8950-9
[1. Sisters—Fiction. 2. Identity—Fiction. 3. Sexual orientation—Fiction. 4. Shakespeare, William, 1564–1616. As you like it—Fiction. 5. Theater—Fiction. 6. High schools—Fiction. 7. Schools—Fiction.] I. Title.
PZ7.B52859My 2009 [Fic]—dc22 2008050279

First Edition—2009 / Designed by April Ward
Printed in the United States of America on acid-free paper. ∞

1 3 5 7 9 10 8 6 4 2

To Pelle for many little reasons and one big one

MY
Invented
LIFE

Chapter 1

I *raise my mini golf club* and try to focus on the clown's chomping mouth. Other lips are on my mind, though—Bryan's, to be honest. As my eyes wander in his direction, Eva leans in to kiss those lips. Bryan belongs to my sister, a circumstance I'd rather forget. My ball sails over the polka-dotted clown hat and disappears deep into Nowheresville, where the gum wrappers live. Mom bribed us into coming tonight by inviting our boyfriends. Except I don't have one.

If life were one big stage (and it is), this would be the scene where the heroine (me) seethes with jealousy and the desire for revenge. The thick folds of her wool cloak conceal a weapon. She unveils the silvery blade to gasps from the audience and advances toward the doomed couple. O happy dagger!

But the pint-sized windmill in the background is all wrong. It creates a trashy-teen-movie sort of ambience when the scene calls for romantic boudoir. Think Othello taking the life of his beloved Desdemona.

Eva and Bryan's kiss goes on for an eternity. When they finally come up for air, he looks over her shoulder right at me. I choose feigned disinterest over murder and saunter off in the direction of my lost ball. My so-called search leads me to a hidden bench that's perfect for an intermission. I stretch out and close my eyes. Here's what I should've said to Mom this afternoon: "Alas, no miniature golf for me tonight. My allergy to Astroturf, you know. Have your people call my people to reschedule."

A sweet smell hovers over my bench. "Wake up, Sleeping Beauty," Bryan says, brushing my cheek with a half-opened rose.

I am so lying.

There are no flowers for miles around. Actually, the smell bears an unfortunate resemblance to cigarette smoke. When I open my eyes, I see Bryan leaning against a chain-link fence a few feet away. He inhales.

"Are you okay?" he asks through a toxic cloud. The glow of his platinum blond hair in the artificial light haloes his face. A girl needs sunglasses to look at him without hurting her eyes.

"I'm tired, that's all," I mumble.

After his parents divorced three years ago, Bryan broke my heart by moving away from Yolo Bluffs. Last September he came back with his dad, and my romantic dreams were rekindled. Sadly, before he could fall madly in love with me, he succumbed to Eva's perky cheerleader routine. And who can blame him? She *is* amazing in every way. Half the boys at school swoon in her presence. Still, here's my chance to make him notice my less-obvious charms, to make him change his mind.

"You seem out of it," he says, dropping down next to me. I sit up.

"I stayed up too late on New Year's Eve. Mom's grad student party," I say. Inside my head I scream at him, *Are you blind? You picked the wrong sister.*

His smile reveals even teeth, not too big and not too small. The song "Sweet Cheater" runs through my head. My heart pounds out a few extra beats.

"Where's your ball?" he asks.

"I don't believe in balls," I say.

Smoke pours from his mouth when he laughs. I cough. He immediately drops his cigarette and rubs it out with the heel of his white sneaker. "Eva says I should quit."

"You should do what you want."

Personally, I believe smoking compares unfavorably to eating raw banana slugs, and I'm one of the few who's tried both. At least when he kisses Eva tonight his mouth will be tainted by eau d'ashtray. I take comfort in this.

"I can't help it. I'm bad," he says.

"That's your best quality," I say.

In the third grade, I would stare at him for the entire lunch period, spending many dreamy minutes on each dimple. Once Eva helped me write him a love survey: Do you like me? Will you kiss me? Will you marry me?

Bryan filled it out yes, no, and yes. Nothing ever came of it, but my crush lived on.

"Great shot, Eva," shouts the member of the Eva Fan Club known as Dad.

I savor the last moments of our intimate silence until Mom ruins it by yelling, "Roz, where are you?"

"Coming," I yell back.

"Something's up with you," Bryan breathes into my ear. "Call me."

Okay, so he's not totally blind. We stand up and join the others. The moment we appear, Eva grabs on to him, circling her arm around his waist like a noose. Her face gives nothing away. Then again, she's a better actress than I am, and I'm the best.

I poke around Eva the Diva's room the next morning after she leaves for her ballet lesson. I haven't come in here since she got mad at me before Christmas. More than mad. She took the folder on her computer desktop titled Roz: sister and best friend and moved it to trash.

The first thing I see is her journal. I'm not tempted. It rests seductively at the center of her night table, and the latch appears to be broken. Still I don't touch it. Even though she'll never find out. And even though it might reveal why she deleted me from her life.

Okay, then, one little peek.

December 20—Last day of practice before Christmas break. Finally got chorus line routine together. Skipped the cheerleaders' party. Went for walk with Bryan.

The rest reads the same. Maybe TV Land hired her to write a script for *America's Boringest Home Videos.* To be honest, I'd hoped for a confession, a green light to go after Bryan. Something like, "Roz wants that loser Bryan. I'm going to hook up with him to get back at her." But back at me for what? I'm innocent. And I'm not looking for a new nickname—boyfriend-stealing lowlife—either. Still, there are extenuating circumstances to consider. For one, I liked him first. For another, all's fair in love and sibling rivalry.

So that my morning won't be entirely wasted, I close her journal and move on to pillaging her closet. We used to trade clothes constantly, without bothering to ask each other first. When my growth spurt made that impractical, we still shared accessories all the time—BD (Before Deletion), that is. Her new ivory scarf feels soft. I wind it around my neck, lie on her bed so my cheek rests on the angora, and hope for a miracle.

The blue pom-poms hanging on her door look like a pair of punk trolls in need of a haircut. I hate them. Since Eva deserted me for her petite cheerleader friends, I fantasize about slipping bovine growth hormone into their Gatorade. My fave internet advice line says it's normal for sisters to grow apart during high school. True, we live in the same house, go to the same school, and hang with the same theater-geek crowd. The 24/7 thing can wear on a person. Except we didn't grow apart. She dumped me, and it hurts.

Eva is one grade ahead of me, a senior in high school. Even BD we pretty much ignored each other in public by mutual consent. When we were alone, though, she used to tell me everything about everything—who kissed with too much saliva, how she had to wear a hoodie around her waist when her tampon leaked, things like that. She stopped spending time with me around Halloween to hang with Bryan. That always happens with a new boyfriend, so I didn't freak. After Thanksgiving she started acting odd, and then she dissolved and recrystallized into a stranger.

Her door swings open. "Did you forget where your room is?" She tosses her gym bag into the closet. "Oh. Your GPS broke down."

A *National Enquirer* headline flashes before my eyes. LITTLE SISTER TURNS INTO A GIANT ZIT ON BIG SISTER'S FOREHEAD. PICTURES INSIDE. She glares at the scarf. I remove it from my neck and set it on the bed. At least she noticed me.

"What do you want?" she asks.

Bryan. A rare bout of self-restraint shuts me up. My big mouth and my conniving side make a sorry twosome.

"I traveled far from a distant land to wait upon your gentle personage," I say.

She sits on the edge of the bed. "What do you want to talk about, Chub?" The parents mistake her nickname for me as cute, not seeing the jab at my weight. I did plump out in fifth grade before shooting up in seventh, but I lost most of those pounds.

I roll onto my stomach to cover the lingering flab. "Anything. How's cheerleading?"

"Great."

A conversation cannot happen through a glass wall. She sees me fine but can't hear what I'm saying. Maybe louder will work. "Isn't there something in the whole freaking universe we can talk about?" I shout.

"Cheerleading sucks, actually."

This unexpected opening knocks me off balance. My silver tongue and I soon recover. "Did something happen?" I ask.

"It's gotten so competitive."

"You *like* competition." My elbow grazes a hard lump

under her down comforter. Is she hiding something in her bed?

"No I don't. I like to do things well."

"Like thieving boys, you mean."

She loads an angsty CD into her stereo and lowers herself into a plié using her ballet barre next to the supersized mirror. "You mean Bryan?" she says after a few dips. "From whom did I thieve him?"

Like she doesn't know. "Nobody."

I run my fingers along the edge of the mysterious object under the blanket. A book. Before I can read the title, Eva pounces. She's the mountain lion to my jogger, pinning me and wrenching the book out of my hands. The back cover rips off in the struggle. I manage to stand up and hold it out of her reach. She gives up and goes back to the barre.

Expecting smut, I read the blurb aloud for maximum embarrassment factor. "'A beautiful coming-of-age story about a girl who falls in love with another girl and their journey of self discovery.' . . . Oooh, does Bryan know about your side interests?"

Her face flushes red. "As if a cheerleading babe could be a dyke," she says.

"I didn't call you a dyke."

The old Eva would've made a joke of it. *Now you know. Just between you and me and the tabloids, Britney Spears and I are lovers.*

"Andie lent me the book. The stage tech with the eyeliner."

"So she's your secret girlfriend," I say.

"Don't be bitchy. Oh, I forgot. You can't help it."

Overreactionville. Silly repartee has always been our trademark. The oh-so-thin filter between my brain and mouth fails once again. "You're the one who's going off. Maybe you really are gay."

She comes over to where I'm sitting on the edge of her bed. "You guessed my secret. I wanted to tell you sooner," she says, taking both of my hands in hers, "but I was afraid. Do you still love me?"

"More than ever," I say. We embrace. "It's cool having a lesbian in the family." The word *lesbian* rolls out of my mouth like I use it every day.

Another tender moment in the invented life of Roz Peterson.

When I say to Eva, "Maybe you really are gay," she casts me a scornful glance.

"Reading a book about lesbians doesn't make you a lesbian," she says.

My foot taps the floor. When I force it to stop, the other foot takes over the job. "I know that," I say. "So why did Eyeliner Andie think you'd be interested?"

She pitches her voice low and sweet. "How would I know, Chub?"

I'm not one to give up, especially when common sense dictates I should. "Maybe she has a crush on you."

"Go away and bother your imaginary friends."

"What about Carmen?" I ask. Carmen is Eva's best friend and cheerleading partner. "She's cute."

"Though parting be such sweet sorrow . . . get out!"

In elementary school Eva used to beg for my company while she practiced ballet. Of course I was sweeter and more pliable back then. When I was nine, I read aloud five volumes of *Little House on the Prairie* while she lengthened her arabesque. At the time, I thought she was doing *me* the favor. On my way out, I turn off Alanis and her whinefest about her self-absorbed life.

"That's mature," Eva says.

I roll my eyes and take Andie's book with me.

Back in my room, I can't sit still. I pick up the glass butterfly that Eva gave me as a thank-you gift years ago. She couldn't stand being the center of attention and proposed running away from home to avoid performing the solo assigned to her in our grade school play—*Pirouette for a Lacewing*. I came up with a better plan. After her grand entrance, I tumbled onstage behind her, somersaulting wildly to distract the crowd.

Maybe Eva really does like girls. That hardly seems like a reason to cut me out of her life, though. And the details don't support my theory. For one thing—if she has the hots for girls, why the long parade of boyfriends? She's run through six in the last two years. And for another—the make-out sessions with Bryan look all too real. The butterfly slips from my hand onto the floor. With a little help from Mr. Superglue, it becomes Frankenfly, a blobby and misaligned creation not unlike my life. I throw the whole thing in the trash.

Chapter 2

Eyeliner Andie's lesbian book is set on the East Coast, where two girls fall crazy in love amidst the geeky world of chess camp. I read the first chapter under the covers with a flashlight like a voyeur. A few pages into it, I emerge from hiding. It's like every other romance novel I've read where a girl falls for a boy and obstacles keep them from getting together—outdated parental rules, misunderstandings, and irritating friends. In this case, outdated hang-ups, prejudices, and irritating friends. Like Eva said, you don't have to be a lesbian to read a lesbian book.

Still, her reaction to the subject has aroused my curiosity. I decide to put her to the test after dinner. The parents conveniently go out for a health-inducing walk through the evening fog, leaving us girls behind to clean up. When they're safely gone, I don my friendliest face. Shakespeare said, "Look like the innocent flower, but be the serpent under't." Translation? A devious mind is a terrible thing to waste.

I ambush her in the kitchen. "What did you think about that sizzling love scene in Andie's book?" I ask. "The one in the pool house."

Graceful Eva drops a waterglass in the sink. It shatters.

"I only read the first chapter," she says.

Here's what she should've said: *Juicy. Who would you cast in the movie version? Ashley or Mary-Kate?*

"Let me read it to you while you load the dishwasher," I say, as if nothing strange just happened.

"Nice try. Get me to do all the work."

Her voice comes out as thin as the watery juice Mom served me during my pudgy phase. My suspicion radar registers a second blip. I pretend I didn't hear her, run to my room, and return with the book.

"Dang. I can't find the pool house scene. Good read, though. It's hip and edgy just like it says on the back cover. You're missing out."

Eva doesn't answer. She stretches slowly like my cat, Marshmallow, when I brush her off the kitchen counter—a stretch that says she meant to be on the floor all along.

"I'm tired," Eva says. "Tell the parents good night for me."

After her exit, I resist the urge to break a few more glasses. The counter needs a thorough wiping. I pretend not to notice. Life PD (Post Deletion) would be easier if my best friend, Sierra, were here. She moved to a tiny village in Guatemala five months ago with her anthropologist parents and lives out of email range except for rare visits to town. No new best friend has stepped forward to fill her cute Uggs. So I hang out with the theater-geek crowd, a loose confederation of friends and enemies. Friendship Lite.

Back in my room, I go online to join the nightly e-chat. Eva is not on.

DulceD (Carmen): tryouts monday . . . any1 red the play

She means our spring play, *As You Like It* by William Shakespeare.

SkateGod (Bryan): i don't believe in monday

DulceD: LOL

D-Dark-O (Nico, a theater geek of minor talent): i don't believe in red

Isis (me): i don't believe in shakespeare . . . the horror, the horror

Sierra picked my chat name. She said that goddesses are tall too.

DulceD: the horror, the horror is from joseph conrad

She fancies herself head and shoulders smarter than the rest of us, a tower of intellect just because she's taking a few AP classes.

Isis: joseph who? the hell cares

I meant to suck up to her so she would share all Eva's secrets with me. Too late.

DulceD:

SkateGod: i'm trying out 4 orlando

DulceD: rosalind is perfect 4 u roz-alind . . .

Roz is short for Rosella, actually. What were Mom and Dad thinking when I was born? To be fair we should be allowed to rechristen our parents when we turn sixteen. I choose Gethsemane for Mom and Elmo for Dad.

DulceD: go for it!

Isis: ?????? isn't rosalind the lead . . . ?

Most days Carmen would kill—or worse—for the lead, so she's being sarcastic. Or is she? A theory pops into my mind—Theory X. Playing Rosalind won't be good for Carmen's new sexy image. Last year she dressed like a nun, but this year she does all her clothes shopping at Sluts-R-Us. And in the play Rosalind pretends to be a man in almost every scene. Carmen wants a role of the tight-bodice variety so that her boobs can look like pears on a platter offered up to the audience.

When I catch my reflection in the full-length mirror on my door, a darker theory suggests itself—Theory Y. Though I'm not exactly fat, the less tactful sort of person uses the word *solid* when referring to me. My waist is a straight line, to be honest. Carmen thinks that I can play a woman pretending to be a man more convincingly than she can.

So what? My lovely curves are more hidden than hers. Shedding a few pounds shouldn't be difficult on the right diet. I've been thinking of going vegetarian, anyway, since reading a gory article on slaughterhouses. Bryan IMs me outside the chat.

Him: i need 2 talk 2u

Omigod. He loves me after all. I don't want to appear as eager as I feel, so I leave him hanging.

Isis: carmen . . . dennis is perfect 4u . . . go for it

Dennis has two lines in the play.

DulceD: don't b bitchy

DulceD: o, i forgot . . . u can't help it

Poor girl can't invent an original insult to save her life. I'll show her how it's done. Of course the Elizabethan curses from the generator I downloaded aren't exactly original either, but no one has to know.

Isis: don't be a hedge-born clack-dish . . . o, I forgot . . . u can't help it

Hedge-born clack-dish means lowly blabbermouth. I can almost see Carmen sweating as she frantically checks Dictionary.com to figure out what I just called her. Before she can fire back another volley, I leave the chat. Our argument is pointless anyway. Eva always gets the lead. And it's about time to answer Bryan's private message to me.

Me: what about eva?

Him: what about her? call me.

After several heart-pounding, sweaty-palm minutes, I call his cell. No answer. My curiosity grows like a mosquito bite begging to be scratched. Does his message have anything to do with Eva liking girls?

Though I'm SO NOT New Age, Sierra introduced me to Ouija for answering life's more pressing questions. I draw the curtains, light a candle, and sit cross-legged in front of the computer. The Ouija Web page cues me to begin.

"Is Eva a lesbian?" I chant, typing as I go.

Under the gentle pressure of my fingertips, the mouse stays put. I picture Eva with her arms around Angelina Jolie. The mouse drifts upward. I open my eyes. The cursor hovers between yes and no. I shut my eyes. My mental picture changes to Bryan in a yellow tank top with me leaning against his perfect pecs. The mouse jumps to yes.

There's my answer.

My bed doubles as a trampoline, which is a good thing because my screechy nerves need some jump therapy right now. On the third bounce, my hair brushes the ceiling and a crunching noise starts up inside my mattress. I drop down onto my back and kick up my legs for a while. Eva is as familiar to me as the lines of overlapping plaster over my bed—BD that is—so it bothers me that I don't understand her. We used to be a team. Well, almost.

One little imperfection got in the way of our perfection; it turns out that Eva is better than me at everything. I solved that by dropping out of choir, ballet, and tap. True, I could've taken up obscure activities—bassoon recitals or spelling bees—but why bother? Theater changed all that. I fell in love with the stage at first sight. Eva's superior acting skills failed to diminish my passion for it. She could have Gretel as long as I could be the evil stepmother.

Then I beat her at something without even trying. One fine day I got breasts, and not the Ping-Pong ball variety. I thought I'd get my period first too, until I found a box of tampons in her room. "What are these for?" I asked.

"Guess," she said.

"Just in case?" I asked.

She laughed and shook her head.

"For cleaning your ears?"

"Right on the second try."

It was an obvious lie, even back then, when I wanted to believe her. I'll ask her why someday . . . if we're ever friends again.

By the morning of the next day, I need to talk to someone. Either that or commit myself to a home for girls with excessive and neurotic nervous mannerisms. I cross the gopher-infested field that separates my house from Sapphire's. Sapphire is the coolest adult for miles around and my drama teacher. Though she's the same age as Mom, they have nothing in common. Mom drives a Volvo, while Sapphire tools around in her lemon yellow VW bug. Sapphire chose a new name for herself when she became an adult. But when I suggested Gethsemane to Mom, she refused to consider it.

As I near Sapphire's house, a Grateful Dead tune comes at me through the open window, along with an unpleasant smell. I let myself in. I find her standing in front of the stove stirring an enormous pot of soup, her bare feet on a patch of floor where the linoleum has worn through. A full stereo dominates the counter where ordinary people put their microwave.

"Stay for lunch," she says, holding out a spoon for me to taste.

The odor—reminiscent of animal hair and toenails—convinces me that the time has come to adopt my new vegetarian diet. "I don't eat meat," I say.

"Groovy. Since when?"

"Since now," I answer.

She laughs. "You don't know what you're missing."

I sit at the kitchen table—a mint green Formica thing from the fifties. A small shelf above it serves as a makeshift altar where the Buddha and the Virgin Mary rub shoulders. Her kitchen has been my haven since forever. I spin the stool, kicking off from the table leg while exhaling slowly like I learned in the meditation class Sierra and I took together.

"So what's the big secret?" Sapphire asks. She can read my mind but never judges. I confessed to her (and her only) when I cheated on a history test last year. She supported me through my kleptomania phase, too. I think of her as a sounding board for my new ideas, a focus group for my new product lines.

"Bryan," I say. "He made a pass at me."

Sapphire pats my hand. If she were Mom, she'd act like a squadron of fighter jets just buzzed the kitchen. "And what did you do?"

I take another deep breath. "Nothing. He's Eva's boyfriend."

"Very mature," she says.

Sigh. My test failed. Even free-spirited Sapphire believes that going for Bryan would be immature.

"I have the perfect balm for your aching heart," she adds. She lowers the volume on the stereo and puts a finger to her lips. I catch guitar strumming from her back room.

"My sister's son is visiting me," she says. "Jonathan's a senior and a hottie too."

"You have a sister?"

Sapphire has never mentioned this before. The omission

raises goose bumps on my arms. When Eva and I were little, I dreamed we would grow up and live together in the same house. Later on I accepted we would just be neighbors. Could we grow apart so profoundly that she wouldn't mention me to her friends? I don't respond well when people strip me of my delusions. Like the time my best friend in the second grade informed me that the Tooth Fairy didn't exist. I hid under her bed and cut off the pink mane of her My Little Pony.

"Would you mind showing him around?" Sapphire asks. "How about tomorrow after tryouts?"

"If Jonathan's a senior, why isn't he in school?"

For a moment she looks like a person choosing between brands of laundry detergent. I'm guessing she's deciding how much to tell me. "He got into a spot of trouble after an ugly split with his girlfriend. Nothing big, but there was talk of suspension. My sister worked it out so he could transfer here."

"You want me to date some juvenile delinquent head case? What did he do?" My elbow collides with the vase of flowers on the table.

Sapphire rights it quickly and tosses a kitchen towel on the puddle. "Nothing terrible. And it's not a date." The guitar music stops. A small thud from the back room shakes the little house.

"Why not introduce us now?" I ask.

The next thud suggests overturned furniture.

"Later," she says, ignoring the racket. "I wouldn't ask if I thought you couldn't handle it." She turns up the music again.

The noise from the back of the house stops. I launch

the next test. "There's something else going on . . . with Eva."

Sapphire tilts her head to show she's listening.

"I think she's a lesbian."

"That's way far out," Sapphire says. "And so cool she can talk to you about it."

Freeze scene.

When I say, "I think she's a lesbian," Sapphire's face darkens. Think computer screen when the hard drive crashes. Soup scum slides down the side of the pot and hisses in the fire. She stands up to lower the flame.

"It's just a theory," I add, faltering a little.

"It isn't appropriate to talk like that about your sister's personal life," she says.

Appropriate? Sapphire sounds positively parental. I jump off the stool, and my hip accidentally bumps the table. The vase falls over again, rolls, and smashes to the floor.

Sapphire hands me a broom and dustpan. "You really had it in for that vase," she says. "It wasn't that ugly."

I don't laugh. Sierra would call it instant karma for talking about Eva behind her back. I call it bizarre.

Sapphire stirs turmeric and cumin into the soup as if nothing happened. I finish cleaning up the mess. "I'd better go," I say. "You know, practice my lines one last time."

"Are you okay?"

"A little nervous about tomorrow."

"With your talent, Shakespeare will be a stroll in the park."

"Thanks," I say.

When I make it outside, I count up my losses—Sierra,

Eva, and now Sapphire. That doesn't even take into account the drought in Boyfriend Land. I see loneliness in my future. Except for a nondate with a quasi punk who probably hates girls based on a warped relationship with his evil ex-girlfriend. That's when I notice strange objects strewn below the open window alongside the house—clothes, an empty suitcase, and an office chair. So he's a performance artist too. I'd title his installation Life Sux Yolo Bluffs Sux More. At least my nondate with Jonathan won't be dull.

Chapter 3

Back home Mom is out with Eva, and Dad is on the phone. After an unfulfilling lunch of raw broccoli and carrots, I log on to chat with someone. Sadly, it's dead in Electron Land. Maybe everyone got boyfriends for Christmas. Anyway, I need more time to obsess about the incident at Sapphire's house. I wish I could Google the inside of her head. Since that's not possible, I Google gay teens. The first site features a coming-out story by Jaylee.

> By the time I was eleven I knew I was different from other girls, and it scared me. So when my best friend chased me around the garden, I pretended my pounding heart was from running so hard. By high school I admitted (to myself) I was attracted to girls. The pressure kept building inside me, until one day my friends asked me a question about the prom, and I started to cry. When they freaked, I blurted out, "I think I'm a lesbian," expecting that to be the end of everything. Instead they surprised me! They had guessed already and were glad I finally told them.

The story moves me so much, I devour a second one, and then another, and another—like Pringles until the tube is empty. Coming out doesn't sound half bad. I'm even a little jealous of some of these girls. For one thing, I wonder if *my* so-called friends would be that supportive. For another, these girls get to be themselves for the first time in their lives, and it's a joyous occasion for the most part. I print the best stories for Eva because they might give her courage to be true to herself.

In case she *is* a lesbian.

Auditions for the play are tomorrow after school. I should be practicing my lines, but Andie's book calls to me with a siren's song. Always put off till tomorrow what you can do tomorrow. I read the book to the end. After a few teary scenes, the other chess geeks come to their senses, embrace the lesbian lovebirds, and throw a dance party where they all dress as their favorite chess piece. I love happy endings.

Since I'm already in procrastination mode, I scour my closet for an outfit with good juju for tomorrow. Unfortunately, my most flattering ensemble—scoop-necked top, floral miniskirt, and velvet leggings—doesn't say shepherdess. Then it hits me. I should take Carmen's "advice" and try out for the lead. While Dad's still on the phone, I borrow a casual button-down shirt and tie from among his work clothes. Then, standing in front of my mirror, I read the lines from the play where Rosalind dresses as a man.

A boar spear in my hand; and—in my heart,

(*I adopt a warrior's pose.*)

Lie there what hidden woman's fear there will,

(*I thrust out my jaw.*)

We'll have a swashing and a martial outside,

(*Where did I leave my sword? I'm always forgetting it under the seat in some café.*)

As many other mannish cowards have. . . .

I remove the tie, unbutton the shirt three notches, and layer with a cute vest. Better. Bryan won't find me attractive if I'm too mannish on the outside. Still, I would do anything to play Rosalind. A tattoo on my lower back—a snake, maybe—or a strategic facial piercing would toughen my image without sacrificing sex appeal. Unfortunately, Mom flips whenever I mention needles and skin in the same sentence. My hair isn't quite right, either. I test the blade of my sewing scissors against my thumb. Not salon quality, but good enough.

Mom suffers from classic bad timing. I wonder if showing up at the wrong moment is an innate talent or a skill she's been developing. Just as the last of my long, auburn tresses hits the rug, she yells from the living room, "I'm home!"

My reflection sneers at me—"Got a little carried away, did we?" When I hear *chhhh* coming from the shower, I sneak past the kitchen with a towel around my head. Gethsemane spots me before I make the front door. Must be Elmo in the bathroom.

"Why are you wearing a turban?" she asks.

I can't think of a good lie. "I joined a cult," I say. "I'll be home before dinner."

"Not wearing that on your head," she says. Parents

should be required by law to listen to themselves so they can hear how condescending they sound.

I take off the towel as ordered. Her reaction deserves the horror movie hall of fame. If this were my cue, I would look behind me and discover a slimy monster of gigantic proportions, saliva dripping off its daggerlike teeth.

"Does this have anything to do with that thing between you and Eva?" she asks.

I swear Mom has barely glanced at me in the last two weeks. Where does she get this stuff? Maybe she really does have eyes in the back of her head. Maybe she bugged my room.

"What thing?" I say. "I was fooling around with a new look."

Mom drives me to Hair Central, where styling guru Miranda does her best to even out what's left. My hair ends up very short, except for a fringe in back that I insist upon based on a lesbian rocker hairdo I saw on the Net. I ask Miranda for some green highlights. She clicks her tongue at me.

"Earth tones are the style this year," she says.

How would she know? Her tongue isn't even pierced.

On the drive home, Mom brings up the topic we've both been avoiding.

"Why did you cut off your hair?"

"I felt like a change. And I'm a vegetarian now, too," I say, employing a simple sleight of hand. Look at the egg. Now it's gone. See the pretty silk handkerchief.

"What brought that on?"

I pinch the roll at my waist. "I'm tired of being fat."

She shakes her head at me. "Your weight is healthy."

I don't want to be healthy; I want to be sexy. "Did you know that they raise pigs in pens so small they can't turn around?" I say.

I can tell from the way she presses her lips together that she will say something reasonable, like we rarely eat pork anyway. We pull up to a red light, and she turns to look at me. I roll my eyes as a preliminary rebuttal to her future argument. She surprises me by saying something entirely different.

"I didn't try vegetarianism till college," she says. "You're a little early."

We get home and choose a recipe together for dinner. While I chop the veggies, she makes the sauce. After a while I admit to cutting off my hair for tryouts, neglecting to mention my new fascination with coming-out stories and how that may have influenced me. Nor do I say a word about my Eva-is-a-lesbian theory. She thinks I went too far cutting my hair for a role I haven't gotten yet, but seems satisfied by the quarter truths I tell her.

"All's well that ends with a cute haircut," she says, and I laugh like a good daughter should.

I set the wok on the table in front of Dad. "Where's Eva?" I ask.

"With Bryan," Mom says.

Well, lah-di-dah.

She misinterprets the look on my face. "You'll find a boyfriend like Bryan someday," she says.

No, Bryan will be my boyfriend someday.

"I don't think Bryan's so great," Dad says.

If Dad had his way, there would be no boyfriends until we finished graduate school.

"Although anybody would be better than your last boyfriend, Prince Charmless," he adds, winking at me. Obviously he forgot that Eva went out with Prince Charmless first.

"Roz decided to go vegetarian," Mom says. She fills his plate.

"Cool," he says.

He's not one to criticize hot food set in front of him, with or without meat. Both of my parents like to cook, but only on weekends when they aren't tired out from work. Unfortunately, we're a family who'd rather eat out in a town with four mediocre restaurants.

"Your next play is *Wind in the Willows,* right?" Dad says.

"I told you we're doing Shakespeare."

Dad has "gotcha" written all over his face. "The new hair and the new diet," he says, holding up a bamboo shoot. "I thought you might be auditioning for lead beaver."

"Ha, very funny." I flick my new tail. "A person who hasn't changed his hair for twenty years wouldn't understand." Dad's retro hippie mop is the perfect complement to his ancient Jerry Garcia sweatshirt.

"You both have adorable hair," Mom says.

She stands up to close the new drapes against the prying eyes of P. Tom, our very own neighborhood perv. P. Tom is big news in Yolo Bluffs, the most excitement we've had since the peach blight two years ago. No one has caught him yet, but he leaves traces—extra-large Birkenstock footprints and Juicy Fruit gum wrappers by our windows.

Eva finally comes home sans Bryan. "Didn't he want cocoa?" Mom asks.

"School night." Eva collapses on the couch.

"He's such a good boy."

I point at my new hair. Eva looks away, and I can feel desperation like a screw tighten one more turn in my chest. Do I have to pierce my nose with a small yet tasteful spear to get her to notice me?

"Well, do you like it?" Mom says, oblivious to Eva's snub.

My sister smirks in my direction at last. "Is it a mullet?"

I imagine a big fish growing out of the top of my head, though I know a mullet is also a hairstyle. "We all can't be as boring as you," I say and then exit.

Back in my room, I dial Bryan's cell. I have the good sense not to call him when he's with Eva. This time he picks up.

"What was the big secret last night during chat?"

"My dad's girlfriend moved in with us," he says.

"Lucky you."

"I guess." I imagine his beautiful hair splayed across his pillow as he talks to me. "Except she's mean. And she hates me."

"How could anyone hate you?" I reach for the photo of him I keep stashed under my bed and kiss the curve of his smiling lips through the glass.

"She told Dad to confiscate my skateboard . . . just because I forgot to water her dumb plants."

"Did he listen to her?" Bryan's skateboard is like an appendage. Taking it away would be the equivalent of cutting off one of his feet.

"No, but he doubled my chores."

"Poor baby," I say.

"Want to wash his car with me tomorrow after tryouts?"

I could tell him about my date with Jonathan to see if he gets jealous. Then again, I haven't met Jonathan yet. He might have a giant *L* for loser blinking on his forehead, for all I know.

"I don't know," I say.

"It would be fun. You, me, soap, and a hose."

I wish Eva could hear how he talks to me when she's not there.

Chapter 4

Mom hovers at the fringes of my life. She's a vegetable crops professor at UC Davis. The long commute and the "publish or perish" credo of the university keep her busy. Combine that with Eva's constant stream of performances, recitals, ad nauseam, and sometimes weeks can slip by without her noticing me. Which means I get away with a lot, barring the obvious stuff like hacking off my hair. A few times a year, she drives us to school. Today is one of those days. When I slide into the backseat, she frowns at me.

"Is that Dad's shirt?"

I pretend to misunderstand the question. "I told you. I'm going for a new look," I say. "If you paid attention to fashion, you'd know button-down shirts are the rage."

Eva hops into the front seat. Her neon pink fiesta skirt glows through the fog like flower petals strewn across a muddy lake.

"Look how perky you are," Gethsemane says.

The word *perky* makes me ill. Mom passed Parenting 101, so she never actually says, "Why can't you be more like Eva?" Still, it's pretty obvious she thinks it.

I stick my finger in my mouth, the universal gag sign. "I don't believe in perky."

Eva laughs. "You look classy in a man's shirt," she says, doing an impersonation of the old Eva for Mom's benefit.

After we de-SUV at Yolo Bluffs High, I rush to the bathroom to adjust my new look. Undoing yet another button helps. When I enter homeroom, Mr. Beltz yammers away at the front of the class, oblivious to my tardiness. Homeroom mixes juniors and seniors, an experiment dreamed up by administration, which explains why Carmen and I are in the same class. Today she's clad from cleavage to ankle in skintight black. How nineties is that? Okay, I'm jealous because her outfit shows off her olive skin and tiny Latina waist. Black makes my skin look like uncooked chicken.

I sit down in the empty seat next to her. "Hey, Carmen, nice earrings." I'd rather slap her around than suck up, but honey catches more vermin. "Do you know what's going on with Eva?"

Carmen's eyes widen when she takes in my new coif. "Yikes. Did you have a close encounter with a low-flying helicopter? Or is your lawn mower possessed?"

"Har-dee-har. My mom likes it," I say.

Carmen extracts a long strand of her lovely black hair and nibbles on the tip. It makes the point rather effectively without a single eye-roll. I don't like the direction this conversation is headed. I return to my original mission.

"Eva's been acting a little strange, don't you think?"

"You're rubbing off on her, I guess," Carmen says.

I punch her arm—lightly, of course. "Has she said anything about me?"

"No."

"What's the big secret?"

Carmen's eyes harden. "I'm not playing your asinine game, whatever it is."

Frustration at my failure sets in. "The SATs are so over," I say. "You can stop using the ten big words you learned for the test."

That came out nastier than intended. It's not entirely Carmen's fault that she uses uppity vocabulary. Her mom made her take three SAT prep classes. Then again, I don't need to tiptoe around her. When it comes to dueling, the point on Carmen's rapier is almost as sharp as mine.

"I prefer the taciturn Roz to the garrulous one," she says. "Or do I mean verbose? No, loquacious."

Which is pretty funny, actually, but I'm not in the mood to let her win this conversation.

"Nice top," I whisper. "Were they out of your size?"

"Don't be a *sheep-biting moldwarp,*" she says.

Dang. She found the online Elizabethan curse generator too. While I ponder my next insult—*sour-faced malignancy* perhaps—the sharp crack of wood against desktop startles me into looking up. Mr. Beltz shakes his medieval wooden pointer our direction. "Christmas is so over, girls. Do I need to separate you this morning?" He's the original Grinch.

"We're done talking," I concede graciously.

Your typical theater geek spends the lunch minute hanging around the school theater (a converted barn), attempting to outperform the other theater geeks. Whoever can do the best impersonation or pop out the funniest line from a play claims the most attention. More talking happens than listening. Most drama types would rather plumb the depths of hell than set foot in the cafeteria. Eva crossed over to the other side, though, when the cheerleaders started eating there.

Today I skip both options in favor of the library computers. Our stray mutt—a mascot of sorts for Yolo Bluffs High—accompanies me. After he stepped into a bucket of blue paint last year, someone dubbed him BlueDragon from a video game. The name stuck, though he's more round-nosed dope than fierce serpent of the sky. My special relationship with BlueDragon comes from our shared social status. When Sierra left, I drifted between groups during lunch. Everyone acted friendly toward me and would give me a few pats on the head, but I never felt welcome to stay long. Maybe I have doggie breath, too.

In the library I take surreptitious bites of marinated tofu while keying in my get-Carmen project. The resulting page is perfectly wicked. Some rise by sin, and some by virtue fall. Translation? Good behavior is for losers. Before school lets out, I sneak a copy of my dastardly deed into Sapphire's office.

Soon after the last bell, every drama wannabe piles into the Barn. The old plank walls are covered with movie posters and funky tapestries. Nothing can mask the faint but permanent odor of anxiety, the underarm kind. Slanted light from the window illuminates the dust kicked up by herds of jittery feet. Before Sapphire starts with the actual auditions, she introduces us to her nephew from Bakersfield.

I'd pictured Jonathan as a minor badass sporting a

torn denim jacket and a sexy eyebrow stud. Instead, his retro shirt, brown corduroys, and Afro give him the look of a *GQ* saint. Sapphire didn't lie about his looks; he's a hottie through and through. But she neglected to mention a minor detail. He's African-American, which she is not.

Bryan reads first for the dashing Orlando. In seconds, I fall under his spell. He practiced a lot, and it shows. I take a bite from my high protein bar, careful to chew with my back teeth to prevent unsightly spots when I smile. The bar is gritty and doesn't satisfy my real hunger. Two freshman girls whisper in the seats in front of me, oblivious to my presence.

"God, he's cute."

"He has a girlfriend."

And a better girlfriend waiting in the wings.

"Besides, I saw him at the movies last weekend *with his parents.*"

"That's so gay!"

I wait until Bryan finishes his reading to drop my notebooks on their heads. They shriek appropriately.

"Oops." I gather up my scattered things. "I didn't see you there."

I slip outside to review my lines one last time. We don't have to memorize for tryouts, but acting tends to go better if you aren't forced to squint down at a paper and stumble over complex phrasings. Besides, Eva always memorizes the scene ahead of time. Learn from the master, I say. When I hear Jonathan's voice carry across the theater, I hurry back in.

Jonathan is good, terrifyingly good. His voice has authority without being loud. He moves across the stage with an athletic grace, drawing me in with a quiet magnetism. If he were reading for the lead role, he would snag it in a heartbeat. I notice Bryan's jaw hanging down to the floorboards. Poor boy.

Nico reads next. His straight black hair cascades over his face and twitches every time he blinks. I feel bad for him because nobody could look good up there after Jonathan. It doesn't help, though, that he stands like an oak tree bent from years of battering winds. And that no one can see his eyes. He usually goes for roles that don't require much emoting.

After Nico reads, Sapphire calls for Rosalind hopefuls. That's when I notice Eva's absence. Omigod. Maybe she wants to give us mere mortals a chance at glory. A more likely theory? She was abducted by aliens. Carmen hastens onto the stage because she always wants to read first. Today it will be her undoing. She takes *my* handout from the top of the stack and runs her fingers through her hair. After a few well-delivered lines, she falls headfirst into my trap.

"So was I when your Highness took his pukedom," she says. Amid snorts of laughter, she repeats the line. "So was I when your Highness took his *dukedom*." She continues reading, her voice infused with indignation. "My father was no *prostitute*." We erupt again.

"Cut," Sapphire says. She passes a fresh handout to Carmen. "From the top."

Carmen plows through the rest of the scene without error, though she fails to capture Rosalind's gentle humor. She gives me a triumphant look as we pass on the side stairs, me on my way up, her on her way down.

"Sweet revenge will be mine, *fen-sucked ratsbane,*" she says in a low voice. Her face is a mask of pleasantry. Translation? Copycat Girl thinks she can outwit *me*.

I shrug it off and take center stage. Immediately my body goes rigid. Think Popsicle with a cute quasi-masculine haircut. Every audition is the same. I jump off the cliff and plummet toward the sharp rocks below. Before I hit the ground, my wings unfurl and I can fly.

"You're on, Roz," Sapphire says.

I fix my gaze on the empty seats in the middle of the theater. The only flying that occurs is that of my lines flying right out of my head.

Sapphire cues me. "Why, cousin, why, Rosalind! Cupid have mercy, not a word?" She fans herself with the handout I refused. I look at it longingly.

Carmen heightens the humiliation by reciting my first line from the peanut gallery. "Not one to throw at a dog."

"Not one to throw at a dog," I repeat.

Carmen would make a perfect yip-yap dog, the kind that lives on her owner's lap. Thankfully, the image cheers me up, and my lines come back in a rush. Soon I am Rosalind, daughter of the banished king, telling off my overbearing uncle. When I finish, Sapphire leaps to her feet.

"We've found our Rosalind!" she bellows amid appreciative hoots from the audience.

I bow to the thunder of stamping feet.

Hit the back button.

To be honest, no one appreciates my talents as much as I do. When I finish, Sapphire stands and says, "Good work, Roz. Who else is reading for Rosalind?"

I slouch in a front-row seat ready to pick apart the performances of my competitors. Eyeliner Andie sidles onstage like a ghost crab, and that surprises me. Techies usually have no interest in acting. They tend to dress in black, lurk in the shadows, and talk softly. Andie fits the type perfectly.

Except for her clothes. They scream to be noticed. Her ensemble today pairs a neon orange top with low-slung, button-studded pants that flare at the knees. A single streak of magenta slashes through her black hair, which matches her eyeliner. Flakes of mascara speckle her cheeks. I'd call her look neo-Goth shabby chic. There's a rumor that she's a lesbian.

She reads well, and I clap with the others when she finishes.

At that moment Eva races into the Barn.

"I'm sorry I'm late. A friend had an emergency. Can I still try out for Rosalind?"

Sapphire waves her up onstage. Carmen looks like I'm feeling, gray from head to toe with disappointment. She doubles over on a bench with her head down between her knees, ignoring Eva for the entire reading. This freaks me out because I've never seen Carmen act this way. As Eva dances down the stairs—not a trace of gloat on her face—Carmen stands up like a zombie to block her way.

"You promised! You said I could have the lead for once."

"I never said . . . you didn't . . . I didn't . . ." Eva goes pale.

My sister has talent, but even Bette Davis couldn't fake shock that convincingly, which makes Carmen the liar here. What game is that girl playing? I barrel into her, pushing her backward hard. She keeps her balance by grabbing onto Bryan. Before I can get in a slap, Sapphire wedges her body between us.

"What's this all about?"

Eva looks genuinely bewildered.

"I hate you," Carmen says.

"Carmen?" Eva says. "I'll quit if you want me to." Tears stand out in her eyes.

Bryan hugs her from the side, and she struggles away from him. "Leave me alone," she says. She runs out of the theater with Bryan right behind.

Sapphire has Carmen by the elbow.

"Eva promised I could have the lead," Carmen says in a low voice, her eyes downcast.

"It's not hers to give," Sapphire says. "Show's over, everyone. Go home. Roz, Jonathan's waiting for you out back."

Wild thoughts bounce around in my brain as I slowly drift toward the door. Something about Carmen's fight with Eva seemed unnatural. Think breast implants, not quite fake, but not exactly real, either.

Chapter 5

Jonathan stands outside holding a white guitar case in one hand. He has a touch of the lonely stray dog about him. It makes me want to take him home.

"Hi," I say. "Pretty dramatic, huh?"

Silence.

When gossip falls flat, move on to flattery. "You were awesome in there. Why didn't you read for Orlando?"

He stands like a statue—a monument to indifference—looking at me blankly. Maybe he has the hearing of a monument as well. I'm too unnerved to repeat myself, so I start walking toward town. He follows.

"Orlando's some rich whitey," he mumbles after a block or so.

Though the engine warning light blinks red, I keep trying. "I guess. Are you ready for the grand tour?" I use excess cheeriness to cover my confusion.

He nods ever so slightly and shifts his guitar case from one hand to the other. I trot out the usual polite conversation starters. "Are you into sports?"

"You wanna know if Shaq's my man? 'Cuz I'm black and tall, right?" His jaw sets to a hard edge. He appears to be clenching his teeth. "Yeah, this here guitar case is where I keep my basketball."

Do-over. He has a vendetta against the world, I tell myself, not against me personally. He doesn't even know me.

"That was lame," I say. "What kind of music do you play? And I'm not assuming hip-hop."

Jonathan's smile—if the thing that happens on his face for a few seconds can be called a smile—shakes my confidence. Maybe he knew me in a past life.

"Oldies," he says. "Anywhere I can plug in?"

The Silo is our local cyber café and teen zone. Before it opened we were forced to hang out at Smelly's (okay, Shelly's), a vinyl diner where aerosolized fat particles mingle with countrified Rolling Stones songs. At Smelly's a cup of coffee comes with a side of fries. I take Jonathan to the Silo. He sets up in the corner while I place our order. When I get back, he's walking his long fingers down the strings of his guitar. The flint in his eyes softens as he plays.

"Would you hold my hand if you saw me in heaven?" he sings, and right then the tension between us dissolves. I imagine him playing me like that, and my pulse accelerates.

At the end of the song I hand him a coffee.

"Can you teach me to play that?" I say, looking at his lips. All I'm asking for is one little espresso-coated kiss to help me forget Bryan.

"Sure," he says. He leans toward me, stroking my back with his long fingers.

My invented life is such a happy one. Too bad reality keeps intruding.

When I ask him to teach me the song, he pretends not

to hear and starts putting the guitar back into the shaggy silver interior of its case. "Please." I make a playful lunge for it.

"Back off," he snarls.

My evil girlfriend theory is gaining ground.

"Why did you play me a love song, then?" I say.

"Clapton wrote that song for his dead son."

"Oh."

"Aunt S told you to hit on me. Am I right?" he says.

Before I can answer, he marches to the door and kicks the doorjamb. "Stay away from me," he yells on his way out. After he's thoroughly gone, I jog home. The cold air plus something else makes my throat ache. I feel repulsive. Sapphire could probably explain it all to me. Unfortunately, I can't tell her about our afternoon at the Silo because she's Jonathan's guardian. At age six, the scarlet *T* for tattletale puts a crimp on your social life. At age sixteen, a bout of flesh-eating bacteria would be preferable.

When I get home, I go straight to Eva's room. The door won't open—a new PD thing—and she doesn't answer when I knock and yell. Mom is working late. Dad tells me to leave Eva alone. I compromise by writing a note.

Hey, Eva. I'm really sorry about Carmen. Can we talk? Something else happened today. Can we talk, pretty please?

I go outside and peer through her window, the concerned-sister version of P. Tom. She's lying facedown on her bed. I tape the note to the glass facing in so she can read it later.

When I check the computer, our chat room is vacant. The house radiates quiet like a museum where the only sounds are from the patrons scratching their heads and the dandruff hitting the floor. I didn't realize until Eva dumped me how many of my so-called friends were actually her friends.

Before I finish sulking, Dad calls me to the dinner table. The T-shirt rock icon of the day is Robert Plant of Zep.

"Serve yourself," he says.

"Is that texturized soy protein?" I ask, pointing at the MadCowDisease loaf.

"It's not vegetarian," Elmo says. "The cow was, though. Before I cooked him."

I heap my plate with brown rice and a few token Brussels sprouts. Since my experience with the banana slug—eating one on a dare during a field trip to the redwoods—overcooked asparagus, okra, and other slimy vegetables are off the menu. Mom comes in as we sit down at the kitchen table.

"I'm home," she sings. "Where's Eva?"

"Hi, Roz. How was your day?" I mutter.

"What was that?"

"Eva's in her room and won't come out," Dad says. "She refused to talk to me."

Mom makes a plate for herself. Her worry lines are deeper than normal. Dad looks at my heap of rice. "Vegetarians eat vegetables," he says.

"If only they could breed veggies to taste like Cheez Doodles," I say.

"A Brussels sprout a day keeps the doctor away," Gethsemane says. "Any idea what's up with Eva?"

"She had a fight with Carmen at tryouts," I say.

As Mom stands up to go to Eva's room, she glances at my barren dinner plate. "There's some tofu in the fridge," she says.

I go to fry some up. At least she bought the firm kind I like.

The phone rings while I'm loading the dishwasher. Mom is still in Eva's room. She picks up the same instant I do. "Hello?" we say in unison.

"Hi, it's Sapphire. Can I talk to Eva? It's about the play."

"Sure," Mom says. "She's right here. Roz, hang up."

"Bye." Ever the serpent under the flower, I hit the mute button, move into the laundry closet, and close the door.

Sapphire: Can we talk about what happened today?

Eva: I got there late because my friend needed me. That's all. I never told Carmen I wouldn't audition for Rosalind.

(Sniffle sounds.)

Sapphire: I'm sorry about your fight. If you think the friend emergency threw off your reading today, I'd like to give you a second chance.

Eva, in a sharp voice: What do you mean?

Sapphire: (Raspy intake of breath) I mean . . . based on the readings as they stand, I will give the lead to Roz.

The phone slips from my hand and falls into the empty washing machine.

Eva: Really?

(Metallic echo.)

Monumental.

I retrieve the phone from the barrel and hit the off button by mistake.

No, this is not one of my crazy fantasies. I hop onto the dryer and dance like those sexy Brazilian soccer players when they score a goal in the World Cup. I wish I could call everyone with the good news. But I can't. For one thing, it isn't official. For another, it would be in bad taste because of the jealousy factor. A smidgen of empathy for Eva dims the glow of my pleasure, but I brush it aside. Does Eva feel rotten each time she beats me out for a role? I seriously doubt it. Still, when I see her online later that evening, I send her an instant message.

Me: talk to me . . .

Me: pretty plz, with sugar, whipped cream + 12 cherries on top?

Eva: i don't believe in sugar

Me: melted chocolate then? *kisses her sister's perfect big toenail*

Me: u r leaving home in a few months . . .

Eva: ok 2moro

Eva: may b

Chapter 6

Since the scooter craze ended years ago, I'm the only person in Yolo Bluffs who still rides one. As I zip to school the next morning, a fantasy bubble reading ROZ, THE NEXT JULIA ROBERTS hovers above my head. The Oscar statue in my hand feels heavier than expected. I crumple my carefully worded acceptance speech and babble an endless stream of thank-yous into the microphone. When I arrive at the Barn door, Sapphire hasn't posted the playbill with my name on top yet. My bubble deflates.

In homeroom, Carmen appears to be absorbed by Balzac in the original French. She takes no notice of me when I sit down next to her. She's wearing a new silver skull earring in her left ear in a desperate attempt to look hip. True confession—I want one too. I restrain myself from asking her where she bought it, though. Mr. Beltz blathers on about college prep stuff completely unaware of the blotch of breakfast matter on his shirt. Maybe I can glean a clue about Carmen's fight with Eva yesterday. I write her a note.

Sup? You read well!

When Mr. Beltz turns toward the board, I flick the folded sheet her way. She scrawls a quick answer and goes back to her book without looking at me. While I read the note, she wraps one of her long black tresses around her wrist like a bracelet. My short spikes turn away in envy.

Desist your banal chatter.

I scribble a response.

My father was no prostitute.

When I slide the paper near her elbow, she knocks it to the floor in what appears to be an accident. The bell rings, and she hurries out without a word.

Eva said she'd talk to me today. I have no intention of letting her wriggle out of it, so I go looking for her at lunch. When I don't find her among the bevy of cheerleader beauties in the cafeteria, I zigzag through every campus hideout I can think of. She's in the gym stretching on the barre.

"What's the deal with you and Carmen?" I say. Small talk is such a time waster.

"We're peachy," Eva says.

"More like rotten peaches. Come on. Just tell me," I say, ignoring every principle of persuasion. Coaxing my sister to talk to me is another PD experience I have yet to grow accustomed to.

"I have no idea."

Though I know this is a lie, I shake my head in a show

of sympathy. "I can't believe what she said at tryouts. That's so messed up," I say.

Eva gives her hamstrings a short break. "I never told her I wouldn't audition for Rosalind."

I recognize progress and tread lightly. "Who had the emergency yesterday?"

"Carrie. She was suffering from a bad-clothes-day-slash-my-boyfriend-is-a-jerk emergency."

Carrie—another pep squad sylph I love to hate. I reserve my comments about Carrie's Lands' End wardrobe and brain-dead boyfriend so that Eva will keep talking to me.

"Maybe Carmen asked Carrie to call you," I propose, "so you'd miss the reading."

"She'd never do that," Eva says. Her voice comes out flat and entirely devoid of conviction. I'm guessing the idea occurred to her, too.

Just as Eva seems about to tell me something, I go and ruin it by sharing my current theory. "Maybe Carmen freaked because of the lesbian thing."

"You're so dense, Chub."

The old Eva would've laughed it off. *So true. Carmen's been jealous since Madonna came into my life, though our affair ended months ago.* Instead she throws a sweaty towel at my face with great force and accuracy. Who is this girl with no sense of humor, and what has she done with my sister? I give up on the diplomatic approach.

"Carmen probably thinks you check her out when she's naked. That you lust for her," I say.

Eva charges me and pins me against the mirror. What she lacks in size, she makes up for in athletic precision.

"Wert thou not my sister, I would not take this hand from thy throat till this other had pulled out thy tongue." Translation? I *am* a tad dense.

"That's Orlando's line," I whisper. "Or were you going to play the male lead?"

The grip she tightens on my neck inspires me to choose my next words with care.

"Unhand me," I squeak. "I take everything back. Maybe I can find out what's really going on with Carmen."

She releases the chokehold. "Okay," she says. "But keep me out of it."

After my last class, I motor to the theater to check for the playbill. Nada. A gaggle of confused theater geeks loiters out front. Bryan and Jonathan are talking, or rather Bryan is talking and Jonathan is listening. Sort of listening while edging away. In fact, Jonathan looks like he'd rather be taking a trigonometry test at the dentist's office. Should I go rescue them?

I hear Bryan say, "Are you adopted? You know because . . . well . . . you're bla—African-American." This is all the proof I need that we're meant for each other. I put my foot in my mouth on a regular basis too, though I don't usually step in a cow pie first.

Knowing from experience about Jonathan's volatility, I wait for him to punch Bryan's nose, which is a little on the pointy side and could use some flattening. Jonathan stuffs his hands in his pockets instead.

"Dad's black, and Mom's white," he says.

"Oh, sorry, bro," Bryan says.

"I'm not your bro."

Abort mission rescue. I walk away, choosing to let Bryan think his awkward moment passed without witness.

An hour later the screen door in the kitchen bangs shut. I put my ear against the wall that separates my room from Eva's. I hear drawers open and close. She must be home, though I didn't hear her car in the driveway. It coughs like a chain-smoking geezer when she shuts off the engine. I go to her room anyway, and find Bryan ransacking her top dresser drawer. He closes it when he sees me.

"If you want to check out some really cute underwear, come to my room," I say. The second the words leave my mouth, I turn away in embarrassment. "Do-over," I yell from the hall.

I go back to the door. "Oh, hi, Bryan," I say. "Did Sapphire post the playbill yet?"

His eyes are sparkling. "Sapphire never showed," he says, playing along.

I sit down on the edge of Eva's bed. He sits next to me so close I can feel his warm breath on my cheek. Suddenly my biggest fear revolves around unsightly earwax.

"How's it going with your dad's girlfriend?" I say to remind him of our last intimate conversation.

"The worst."

"You should ask Nico for advice. His mom has a live-in boyfriend."

"I don't want to talk to anyone else about it. It's too private."

His skin smells of sun-dried wildflowers instead of

cigarettes. The sexy scent soothes me and makes me stupid at the same time. Or at least that's my lame excuse for what I say next.

"Do you know that Eva . . . might be a lesbian?"

He stares at me for a long moment. "You mean she's gay? It doesn't matter. You're the one I've always wanted," he says, wrapping his arms around me.

Total drivel. One too many visits to Bryan Fantasy Land have wrecked my grip on reality.

When I say, "Do you know that Eva . . . ?"

Bryan says, "Eva what?"

"Thinks she'll get the lead in the play."

Bryan looks puzzled. "Of course she will. Slam dunk."

"Doesn't it bother you?" I ask.

He stands up and paces the room. "Going out with the most talented girl at school? No. But I wonder what she sees in me sometimes." He sags like BlueDragon when he gets pushed away from someone's tuna fish sandwich.

"Not true. You're brilliant. You got the lead in *Hansel and Gretel.*"

"That was years ago, and it wasn't Shakespeare."

"You'll be better at Shakespeare," I insist.

He moves in close again. "You're good for me, Roz," he says in a husky voice.

"What are you going to do about it?" I whisper.

He looks at my lips. "I can't."

"Can't what?" If you could see dignity, mine would resemble a well-chewed doggie toy. I feel more humiliated than during my first pap smear.

Eva's car engine coughs. I throw her pom-poms at him, wishing that they were spiky instead of fluffy.

Eva the Diva waltzes in. "What's going on?" she says.

"We were just talking about how perfect you are," I say. "Ciao!"

After retrieving the photograph of Bryan hidden under my bed, I search the back of the closet for the hockey stick Dad gave me, a mistake on his part six Christmases ago. My zeal for the sport far exceeded my skill. Eva went to the emergency room with a fractured toe, and she wasn't even playing. I place Bryan on the floor, raise the wooden stick over my head, and slam down hard. "Take that, you *dog-hearted horn-beast,*" I say.

When I hear Eva's footsteps coming down the hall, I throw my quilt over the shattered glass and lie on top of it one second before she throws open my door. With nary a comment on my odd lounging spot, she perches on the edge of a chair piled with dirty clothes, holding her back as straight as an ice pick. She softens me up with the silent treatment.

"What's wrong?" I picture myself as an innocent daisy.

"You're a villainous contriver." Translation? She knows me too well.

"What?"

"That's Shakespeare. It means you are a sneaky twit. What were you two doing?"

"Nothing," I say softly. Saying too much in my own defense might come off as lying, which, admittedly, I'm doing. "What did he say we were up to?"

"Nothing."

"See?" I reach for my toes to hide the relief on my face.

She sweeps a stack of papers from my desk onto the

floor. "I know what I know." Her lips have a pale cast to them.

Naturally I do the right thing, change the subject by pointing at the literature about gay teens that now blankets the floor. "Did you know that Amelia Earhart was rumored to be a lesbian?" Silence. As the void created by her nonanswer expands, I have no choice but to fill it. "And Margaret Mead. Even Plato."

"Plato was a lesbian?" Eva says.

"ROTFL," I say. The furnace-air dries my throat. If only I could crack open the window, but I don't dare leave the quilt covering up Bryan's mangled picture. "Why don't you want to talk about it?" I say.

"I told you already. It has nothing to do with me." She picks up one of the printouts and tosses it into the trash.

"You shouldn't be scared to come out."

Eva looks at me like I might start spooning applesauce into my ear any minute. "Maybe you're fascinated with this topic because *you're* the lesbian, Roz," she says. "Maybe *you* should come out."

I laugh out loud. Boy-crazy Roz comes out as a lesbian? What a farce. Then I stop laughing. A minute ago Bryan made it abundantly clear he doesn't want me. If I can't have him, I don't want a sorry substitute boyfriend. And girls *are* better than boys, actually. Prettier and easier to understand.

If I came out at school, the limelight would be mine for once. My name would grace the Grand Marquee. ROZ PETERSON starring as the First Lesbian on the Yolo Bluffs HS stage. Sure, rumors float around that so-and-so might be gay, but no one shouts it proudly from the rooftops. I'd have the lead in a play written and directed by me. Pretending to be a lesbian is insane, of course, but as a person of the theater-geek persuasion, I pride myself on occasional acts of insanity.

"You really are considering it, aren't you?" Eva says. Do I detect a shred of admiration beneath her scorn? "You probably think it would make you popular."

"Do not!" I say. I hate that she sees how shallow I am.

"You wouldn't last a day," she says, smiling at the idea of my pain and suffering. "You'd beg the parents to transfer you to a new school within a week. I dare you to try it." She imagines me going up in flames and laughs with genuine pleasure. "Oh, and if you make another move on Bryan, your life won't be worth living." She exits like the divas in the old movies.

I roll off my quilt and bury the remains of Bryan in a brown paper bag at the bottom of my wastebasket. The quantity of broken glass in my life keeps mounting. I wonder what Sierra would make of it.

After dinner I attempt oblivion through chemistry homework. Minutes later, I hurl the offending textbook across the room. My computer signals an e-chat in progress. Tempting, but I must decide something first. I prop my elbows on either side of the keyboard and stare at the blackness outside. To be or not to be (a lesbian)—that is the question. Translation? Even occasional acts of insanity require preplanning.

Mom says to create a list of pros and cons when making a difficult decision. I bet she's never imagined one like this.

THE PROS AND CONS OF COMING OUT

Con: potential razzing by classmates	**Pro:** paving the road for others
Con: no new boyfriends	**Pro:** revenge against previous obnoxious boyfriends
Con: lying	**Pro:** opportunity to hone acting skills
Con: Eva furious at first	**Pro:** will show Eva the way (if she is a lesbian)

I'm an intuitive person, a person ruled by my heart. And at this precise moment my heart churns with resentment. Eva has Bryan wrapped around her petite little finger. Sapphire will give her the lead in the play. Eva will cut me out of her life forever; when I visit her on her deathbed, she'll refuse to see me. Her condescending dare this afternoon grates against my one last nerve. I know this is the right moment to press my impulse-control button, but I can never find it when an impulse has me in its grip.

I ball up the list and toss it into my wastebasket. It hits the inner rim and bounces out, an omen I choose to ignore. I log on to the chat. Eva is there.

> Isis (me): just so u heard it from me 1st, i have a grrlfriend

Not the full coming-out I planned, but oh well. The cursor blinks as the stunned theater geeks take in the news. I'm about to exit when a reply pops onto the screen.

D-Dark-O (Nico): cool

And more follow.

DulceD (Carmen): go for it

SkateGod (Bryan): got a webcam?

The worm!

ItGirl (Eyeliner Andie): grrl from YBH?

Eyeliner Andie usually lurks in the background during chats. I'm flattered to hear from her.

Isis to SkateGod: i don't believe in webcams

Isis to ItGirl: UCDavis freshgrrl, ttfn

After exiting, I don a sexy nightgown from Victoria's Secret and throw on a Fountains of Wayne CD. Dancing calms me. Besides, it's almost impossible to bite your nails while doing the pogo. I picture P. Tom at my window and wonder why the poor guy doesn't hitch south to Los Angeles where he'd be better rewarded for his efforts. Our town motto reads: Orchards, orchards everywhere, dropping rotten fruit.

When Chris Collingwood belts out "Stacy's mom has got it goin' on," I turn up the volume. You can write a song about lusting after your girlfriend's mother. My imaginary grrlfriend at UCD is small potatoes by comparison. When the song is over, I surf the Web to research my role tomorrow. Yes, I've watched *Ellen* reruns and seen Melissa Etheridge on the music video channel, but they're middle-aged lesbians. I need to know how young, hip lesbians dress. While I get nowhere on fashion, Eva IMs me.

Her: what the hell r u doing?

Me: accepting your dare. *thumb on nose and fingers wiggling*

Chapter 7

At four in the morning, the cockroaches and I are awake. The cockroaches, btw, are having more fun. When the sky lightens to pale gray, I revive myself with minty toothpaste and a pathetic fantasy. After my heroic coming-out, Eva sees that the whole enchilada is no big deal. She breaks up with Bryan and tells the world that *she's* the lesbian. For the encore—Bryan serenades me with a ballad he wrote in my honor, begging to be my boyfriend.

Today the curtain will go up on my play, *The Lesbian of Yolo Bluffs High*. Time to resurrect the floral miniskirt and velvet leggings I rejected on Monday. I can be a femme lesbian, at least. Except for the hair. The hours before an opening are always the hardest. Maybe I should invent a new nervous mannerism—a sexy one for a change—like running one finger under my bra strap or licking my lips. Just kidding. Or not. I shake my bosoms at the mirror. I don't like the way they jiggle back at me.

Things get worse. At school someone has scrawled ROZ IZ A LEZ across the front of my locker in dark plum lipstick. Gossip—defying the laws of physics—travels faster than the speed of light. People look at me as if I made a full-blown announcement over the PA rather than a quasi announcement in a locked chat room.

Then things get better. The grind of skateboard wheels on pavement alerts me to Bryan's approach. He slaps my backside in a flirty way as he passes.

"You're still cute, queer," he says. A bluebird of happiness rises in my chest. Bryan Fantasy Land is open for business as usual.

Some things remain the same, only more so. When I plunk down in the seat next to Carmen, she cringes like I'm a half-eaten mole Marshmallow dragged in and plague-infested fleas are about to spring on her.

"You told me to go for it," I say, patting her arm.

"Unhand me, you uncouth maid," she says.

RoZ haZ cootieZ.

When the lunch minute rolls around, I fly down Main Drag Street on my scooter, painting a trail of chrome across the storefront windows. At VideoCorral I ask the twenty-something employee to suggest a lesbian film. I refrain from adding a stupid remark like, "It's for a friend." She scrapes her teeth across her tongue stud while she thinks. Only good recommendations will come out of a mouth like that. She pulls down *Better Than Chocolate*.

I tuck the DVD safely in my bag and roll over to visit Zip-Stop Jenny, a convenience store owner and overt lesbian. We happen to be on a first-name basis because of Mom's moratorium on junk food in the house. I grab some chips from the rack and pour myself a cup of gnarly coffee. I scrutinize Jenny with new eyes while I pay.

"Any gum-buying, Birkenstock-wearing customers lately?" I ask. "P. Tom must have to stock up now and then."

"Just you Peterson girls buy Juicy Fruit these days," she says. "I've been meaning to ask you about that. Learned any 'juicy' secrets about your neighbors?"

I raise my foot to show off my stylish winter boots. "These feet have never touched Birkenstocks," I say.

Jenny leans toward me and waves a hand over my head. "You are one of us, now," she whispers. "We meet after midnight at the stone circle."

Another mythical incident in my invented life.

I wish someone would invite me into a secret lesbian club. When I show Jenny my winter boots, she leans in and lowers her voice.

"The Peeping Tom hit Harrison's place. He must've gotten pretty bored watching reruns of old game shows." Lesbians like to gossip as much as everyone else. Big surprise.

Fifteen minutes into fifth period—it's not my fault the lunch minute passes too quickly—I skirt the soccer field, where Jonathan cuts a sad figure on the damp grass. He looks like a well-dressed version of the Thinker. I veer from the path and drop down next to him.

"Hi," I say.

He scoots away from me like I'm depleted uranium.

"My father was no prostitute," I say.

He cleans his fingernails with the blade of a small pocketknife.

I bottom crawl two yards in his direction. "Did you do theater at your high school in Bakersfield?"

He stabs the blade in the grass between us. "I told you to stay away," he says.

Coming from him, the gesture doesn't seem particularly threatening. I take some nail polish from my bag and touch up a few chips to prove that I'm not the backing-down type. As I blow on my fingertips, BlueDragon ambles over, wagging both head and tail. A gentle elbow to the ribs keeps him from jumping into my lap. Jonathan scowls at me. Obviously he's never experienced the trauma of dog hair in wet nail polish. When BlueDragon curls up next to Jonathan, I leave.

I dash over to the theater after my last class. Still no playbill, but there's a note tacked to the Barn door:

Greetings, aspiring thespians,
I will post roles tomorrow morning.
First rehearsal tomorrow after school.
Thank you for your patience,
Sapphire
P.S. Carmen and Roz, please come see me today at 3:30.

I look at my watch. That's in five minutes. Bryan skids to a stop behind me and props his skateboard against the wall. I ignore him until he grabs me around the waist and lifts me off the ground. "You don't like boys anymore, huh?" he breathes into my ear.

"I didn't say that." We stare at each other.

His eyes are a little too close together for perfection, but who cares? It gives his face character. And it won't interfere with his future as an underwear model. Before anything happens Oak-Tree Nico, Eyeliner Andie, and another girl who acts like Mandy Moore come around the corner. Bryan puts me down—the wimp.

Mandy Wannabe comes right up to me and pumps my hand. "It's so cool that you're, you know, out in the open," she says.

"There's plenty more where I came from," I say, launching my program to eradicate ignorance. "Ten percent of people are GLBT."

"Geebee what?"

"Gay, lesbian, bisexual, or transgender," I say.

Mandy Wannabe lets go of my hand. "Whatever."

Eyeliner Andie has her arms twined around Nico's waist in a girlfriendy sort of way. This casts some doubt on her alleged lesbian status.

Bryan points his chin at Sapphire's note. "What's that all about?"

I shrug. "I guess I'll go in and find out."

Sapphire is at her desk munching on a Greek sandwich, two braids coiled into buns over her ears. I leave the door open like she tells me to. "What's up?"

"We'll see. Carmen requested a meeting."

Just then Ms. Strumpet herself strolls in wearing a skintight top zipped low to reveal cleavage, a miracle of Wonderbra enhancement. I run my palm across my hair spikes.

Sapphire throws her gyro wrapper into the waste bin. "Sit down, girls," she says with unfamiliar gravity.

"I came to rectify an iniquitous injustice," Carmen huffs.

"Come again?" Sapphire says.

"The audition wasn't fair because *someone*," Carmen rolls her eyes in my direction when she says this, "messed with my script. I demand a second chance to read for Rosalind."

So. Despite their fight, Eva told Carmen about Sapphire's phone call. The room fades to gray and breaks into dots. I'm hyperventilating again. I hold my breath until the world bursts into color.

"You're right, Carmen," Sapphire says. "And though Roz read beautifully, I have no choice but to give you the role. You're prettier than her. Petite, too."

Welcome to Roz Nightmare Land.

Fortunately, nothing of the kind happens. Sapphire lets Carmen finish her screed on fairness—which goes on far too long, if you ask me—before saying a word.

"You read well, Carmen," she says at last. "Very well. But Roz has blossomed this year. I want to give her a chance this time."

Carmen jumps out of her seat. "This is my last opportunity to be the lead. I'm a senior. Roz can try again next year." She's annoying, and not just because she can French-braid her own hair.

"You can try again in college," I say.

"It wouldn't be the same without Sapphire's superb directing."

Unchin-snouted foot-licker. Sadly, Sapphire doesn't approve of epithets. So although this one is brilliant, I keep it to myself.

"Girls." Sapphire stretches her arms wide. "You both have long and successful lives ahead of you. This is just one play out of many."

She is so wrong.

Crocodile tears slide down Carmen's cheeks. That girl will stop at nothing to win. Still, I can't help but admire her skill.

"It's my mom," she says. "She believes that cheerleading and drama are interfering with my schoolwork. She said that if I don't get the lead, I have to drop out of the play."

Ouch. Poor Carmen. I mean it sincerely. I'd rather die a painful death than quit drama. If Mom made demands like that, I'd be forced to sneak around behind her back. More than I usually do.

Sapphire hands Carmen a tissue. "You'll get a good role in the play. I can talk to your mom, if you like. Tell her the play will be a flop without you."

"She's not stupid. Just because she didn't graduate from high school."

That's weird. Carmen often brags about her mom's meteoric rise in high tech. She emigrated from Mexico as a teenager and now works as a software engineer for a major computer company. She must be a poster child for night school.

"We'll think of something," Sapphire says.

When Eva the Diva comes home after cheerleading practice, I drag her into my room before she can lock herself in hers. I close the door behind us. She refuses to sit down even after I've dumped the stuff from my chair onto the floor. Instead she stands in the middle of my rug with her arms crossed. I feel like a fisherman that's just reeled in a moray eel by mistake. But it's too late to throw her back.

"Are you trying to piss me off? Is that why you're pulling this stunt?"

Not exactly. I'm doing it because you dumped me. Because Bryan chose you. Because you dared me to.

"I'm just having fun," I say.

"The great activist and champion of causes," she says, "trivializing gays. For fun."

I need a cogent response. "Am not," I say.

Logical arguments are not my forte, especially when I do something I can't explain. She opens my door and makes as if to leave.

"Today wasn't easy for me," I say.

She hesitates, her hand still on the doorknob. "Oh yeah?"

"None of my friends hugged me, not even once." We theater geeks touch a lot—hug, polka around the room, and smoosh cheeks together for pictures.

She shuts the door again and looks at me curiously. Maybe I've turned into a species of arachnid with multiple heads.

"They probably thought I would fondle their breasts," I say.

"You could come clean," she says.

"What if no one believes me?" This doesn't seem like the right time to mention that I'm enjoying the role. Just a little.

"I have an idea." Her eyes glitter with mischief like the old Eva. "Tell everyone that when you were making out with your girlfriend you made a discovery."

I rise to the bait. "What did I discover?"

"Your girlfriend is actually a boy who dresses like a girl. For fun. So you're hetero after all."

I crack up because she's being the old Eva and it feels good. She starts laughing too, but stops so suddenly that I have to wonder if she made a pact with herself never to giggle with me again.

"Just tell the truth," she says in a hard voice.

"Forget it," I say. "I'm not a coward like you."

I feel a déjà vu coming on, at least that's what Sierra would call it. Once Eva and I dyed our hair blue for a football game. Afterward she freaked and washed her hair for two hours straight. We missed the game. She wanted me to wash mine out too before Mom got home, but I said no. I told her I wasn't a coward like her. The shiner she gave me that day matched my hair perfectly.

This time she exits my room like I don't exist. I prefer her fists to her silence.

Chapter 8

Thursday morning before the first bell, the theater geeks—minus Eva—gather in front of the Barn waiting for the long-anticipated playbill. Carmen bumps my shoulder hard like I'm in her way. Lately she's the pimple on the butt of my life. I move over to a spot near Andie where I can study her eyeliner. She has thick lines of indigo around her eyes, and she brushed her lids with two shades of gold. She could be an Egyptian goddess. Note to self: Buy makeup after school.

Jonathan stands apart from the crowd. "Hi," I say to Andie. "Let's go talk to the new guy."

"Let's not," she says.

I drag her over anyway so she can be my shield. "Meet Eyeliner Andie. She's my twin sister," I say. Jonathan looks confused. "Fraternal twins." I turn to Andie. "Did you know that Jonathan hosts his own MTV show?"

He doesn't run away from me this time, and I am grateful.

"Don't look so worried," Andie says, shifting into rare social-butterfly mode, though her ripped jeans say more wind-battered moth. "Roz always acts like this."

I take offense. Andie barely knows me.

"I hear you're into music," she says to him.

"I do a little guitar."

Within seconds, they're gabbing like old friends. Worse still, they don't include me in their conversation. Before I figure out what to do next, Sapphire emerges from the Barn. The throng falls silent. She passes around a box of tissues.

"Take one just in case," she says. "And be nice."

She tapes the playbill to the door, and we all rush in to look. Seeing my name at the top of the list in black and white fills my heart with whipped cream. It's official. Before I can do a victory dance, I notice Carmen's tragic face. Two puddles of black sludge are forming under her eyes. Despite the butt pimple thing, I feel sorry for her.

"You should've gotten the lead," I say. The insides of my cheeks stick to my teeth when I lie. I sling my arm around her shoulders to show I care. She shakes me off.

"It's just an arm," I say. "Not a python."

She smears the wet mascara around her face and joins the group paying homage to Bryan. I follow her. He got the lead, Orlando, who happens to be Rosalind's love interest in the play. Could life get any more perfect?

"I'll bet Eva won't like it when she finds out you have to kiss Roz," Mandy Wannabe says to Bryan. "In the play, I mean."

"Kissing a dyke doesn't count," he says.

Life has a way of flushing perfection down the toilet. I stuff down the upwelling of tears. Eight years ago, my psychology-impaired swim instructor told me I looked ugly when I cried.

"I don't believe in dykes," I say. No one laughs.

"I have a brilliant idea," Carmen twitters like a bird on caffeine. "Roz can play Rosalind as a man, and I'll play Rosalind as a woman." She adjusts her sweater to reveal more skin.

"Ooh la la," Bryan says. He sweeps up Carmen in the classic Hollywood style to kiss her.

Another incident written and produced by Personal Nightmare, Inc.

What really happens? Nothing. When Carmen offers to play Rosalind as a woman and bats her sludgy eyelashes at Bryan, he turns away from her. Here are the facts. Carmen looks good, even with mascara waterfalls running down her face. Bryan loves to flirt. Eva is conveniently absent. So his indifference surprises me. I'm delighted, of course, but confused. We disperse without further ado.

When the lunch minute rolls around, I consider where to go. Theater-geek central seems a less appealing option after Bryan's dyke comment. So I bravely dive into the cafeteria. While in the slop line, I use my peripheral vision to scout for a table that is far, far away from where Eva and her cheerleader lovelies are on display. The cafeteria lady taps her tongs against the vat of shriveled chicken wings to get my attention.

"Oh, frog legs," I exclaim. "My favorite. Do they come with a portobello Cabernet sauce?"

The boy in line behind me gets it, but the server's face doesn't change. Years of standing over bad-smelling steam would dull my funny bone too.

"Aren't you required to serve a vegetarian option?" I ask.

"My name is Clara, and I will be your waitress this afternoon. Would you care to try our potato and chard soup with pesto garnish?" She adjusts the white cloth hanging over her arm.

If only. My five-star fantasy makes my stomach growl.

"This is vegetarian." She taps a bin containing the skeletal remains of green beans.

"I'd like to lodge a complaint," I say.

She cracks a smile at last, but the flavor is more horror flick than comedy. She gestures me to the kitchen behind her. "Ask for Felicia," she says.

Felicia is a full twelve inches shorter than me and exudes the authority of a turbocharged pit bull. A pretty pit bull, despite the plastic bag over her hair, the rubber gloves, and full-length apron. I try the mannerly approach.

"Are you Felicia?"

"Yes." Her look says: *Now you know. Shove off. You're in my way.*

Luckily I own a fake thick skin to wear over my thin one. "I'm Roz. Pleased to meet you." I offer my hand in a friendly way. She looks at it like something I fished from the garbage. "I understand you're very busy. Still, I was wondering. Would it be too much to ask for a vegetarian main course?"

"Try the salad."

I'm making headway. She's gone from one-word answers to three-word answers.

"A person could starve on salad alone."

"Maria!" she yells. "More rolls." After she barks a few more orders, she looks me up and down. Her eyes gleam with what I take to be admiration for my persistence, plus a hint of amusement. "Okay. Feeding all you hungry kids is a lot of work. If you volunteer to work here, I'll think about it."

"Deal," I say.

The way the other women in the kitchen laugh at this is a bit concerning.

I'm three minutes late for rehearsal. The few stragglers in front of the Barn fall silent when they see me. An unattractive pair of boxer shorts—plaid and XXL—flaps in the breeze over the door. A poster board underneath reads RoZ'S SKIVVIEZ. I walk past my so-called undergarment as if it were a silken banner proclaiming LONG LIVE PRINCESS RoZ.

The prank has Eva written all over it. We did one like it in reverse two years ago after her then-boyfriend hooked up with another girl at a party. Except we used a satin thong edged with pink lace. Rehearsal season will be long this year. To boost my confidence for my grand entrance, I imagine myself as Marilyn Monroe in mink.

"I don't believe in underwear," I announce to everyone in the Barn.

Eva looks at me with the same level of interest she'd bestow upon a passing housefly. I land next to Eyeliner Andie. The odor of herbal smoke seeping from her wool coat says she's high.

"Congrats on Audrey," I say. "It's an awesome role."

"Thanks," she says.

When nothing more seems forthcoming, I consider several subtle openers that could lead to mentioning the lesbian chess camp book. "I read that romance you gave Eva," I say at last. Subtlety is one of my lesser talents.

She bites down on a loose press-on nail and yanks it off with her teeth.

"I loved the part where they dressed up like two queens for the costume party," I say.

"What?"

"Never mind," I say. "Have you read anything good lately?"

"*Lesbian Fashion for Dummies.* Your dyke-do," she says, giggling, "was big in 1986."

I tug at the beaver fringe at the back of my head, wishing it would come off like a poorly attached weave. Just in time, Nico rolls our way—a Greek column on wheels. Eyeliner Andie hugs his hand between her cheek and shoulder. His fingers are nice, with well-kept nails squared at the ends. Her hands are tiny by comparison.

Sapphire calls for our attention. "Most of you have heard this speech many times, so I'll cut short the part about my expectations—punctuality, perfect attendance, hard work, respect, and—the big one—no gum."

Bryan saunters to the wastebasket and spits out his gum. Carmen laughs.

"I've just learned from administration that they've hired a contractor to renovate the Barn . . ." *Cheers.* ". . . starting on Valentine's Day." *Two gasps and one boo-hiss.* "We've already lost two rehearsal days this week, so our timetable will be tight. We're using a pruned version of the play, but that still means daily rehearsals, long hours, and additional work at home and on weekends." *Groans.* "I know you're up to the challenge. So let the fun begin!"

I escape to a private corner to eat a few bites of cottage cheese before going onstage. Stomach growls are a major source of embarrassment, third only to passing gas and spitting on fellow actors. Bryan goes on first as the rebellious Orlando under the thumb of his oldest brother. I watch from the sidelines, and my bones soften like a chocolate bar left on a car dashboard in the summer. He should be against the law.

By the time he finishes his scene, there's no part of me left unmelted. I attempt to resolidify because Eva and I are on next. I've already memorized the first act, so I expect to nail Rosalind right away. But when I start speaking, Eva opens her eyes in alarm and shakes her head at me. Did I say my lines wrong? I don't think so. Eva's performance so unnerves me, though, that I hesitate in the wrong places and falter where I should sound confident. Worse yet, midscene I forget my lines altogether.

"I would we could do so . . . forsooth."

Before I can shout for someone to cue me, Carmen recites the entire line perfectly.

"I would we could do so; for her benefits are mightily misplac'd, and the bountiful blind woman doth most mistake in her gifts to women."

On the fourth run-through, Sapphire's patience has run its course.

"Roz. Why are you off book when you don't know your part yet?"

Carmen recognizes the opportunity like a thirsty leech recognizes rosy flesh. "I know the part from beginning to end. Let me play Rosalind today."

Beslubbering canker-blossom. For a second her audacity

takes my voice away, but then the perfect counterattack comes to me in a flash. Sometimes I amaze myself with my own brilliance.

"Carmen, could you please put on a coat," I say. "The problem is . . . you're so sexy I can't concentrate."

Carmen flushes a shade of red so bright that even the whites of her eyes turn pink.

"Roz!" Sapphire says. Stainless-steel sushi knives come to mind. "One more outburst like that and you're history."

My chest aches from the unfairness of it all. Sapphire is turning a blind eye to what's really going on. Can't she see how Eva and Carmen—who aren't even speaking to each other—have teamed up to wreck my performance? Still, I know that neither whining nor witty comebacks will get me anywhere. I take the script she offers me.

The scene runs smoothly after that. By the time Bryan comes to the palace for his wrestling match with Charles, I'm in the zone and can enjoy the part where we fall in love at first sight. I summon him from across the arena. He strides beneath my balcony—just a chair for now—to speak with me.

Me/Rosalind: Young man, have you challenged Charles the wrestler?

Bryan/Orlando: No, fair dykeness. He is the general challenger. . . .

When I open my mouth, nothing comes out. *Et tu, Bryan?*

Sapphire whacks Bryan over the head with her notebook. "Enough!" she says. "What did you all have for lunch? Mexican jumping beans smothered in hormone sauce? Tomorrow the serious work begins. You're dismissed."

As the geeks disperse, I chase after Eyeliner Andie because she's the only one I want to talk to. Normally I avoid waif types that make me feel like a giantess. Fee fie foe, no fun. But there's a difference between her and the others. For one, she lacks that Morning Talk Show Host perkiness I detest. She has this otherworldly quality, like her body is just incidental to her life.

"What did you think of your first rehearsal?" I ask when I catch up with her.

"Interesting." She stops walking and lowers her voice. "Do you want to know who did the boxer shorts?"

"I know already," I say. "Eva."

She nods and shakes her head in an ambiguous Mona Lisa way.

"Then who?"

"You already know," she says. I can't tell if she's being sarcastic. "Does your girlfriend ever come to Yolo?"

"Rarely," I say.

"What's her name?" Her voice has been getting warmer as we talk, approaching tepid.

"Candy," I say without thinking, and then scramble to make my lie more convincing. "Well, that's just her chat name. Actually her name is Carmella. We met on the Web." For one crazy second, I think Andie might ask to meet her. "We kind of broke up," I say. "Long-distance love, you know."

"I know," she says. "See you around."

Chapter 9

Outside the theater, the drizzle brings out the smell of old leaves, eau de decaying maple. I don my cheap plastic rain poncho. Eyeliner Andie has disappeared. She's a spirit girl who can vanish at will. Weirder yet, Nico pops out of nowhere like a gopher from a hole.

"Where's Andie?" I ask because Spirit Girl and Gopher Boy appear to be an item.

He shrugs. "You were great in there," he says. He kicks a rock out of a puddle. "Andie says . . . Andie thought . . . Well, Andie has this idea that . . ."

I grow impatient. "What?"

He studies the water beading on his boot. "Nothing."

Life would be much easier if people's real agendas scrolled across their foreheads as they talked. Of course, in that case I'd be screwed.

"Okay, bye," I say. I leave him there, maneuvering my scooter around the puddles. The drizzle turns to rain. When I look back at him, he hasn't moved at all, not even to put up the hood of his jacket. I wonder what he wanted to tell me.

At home, a dozen vegetarian cookbooks from the UC

Davis library are stacked on the kitchen table. It's sweet that Mom thought of me, but I'm a tad ambivalent about becoming one of her projects. I bookmark a few recipes at random so she'll imagine I spent an hour poring over them instead of plotting ideas how to get back at Eva. Which is what I embark upon immediately after holing up in my room.

The ancient Save the Whales poster on my wall sparks an idea, and I scour my desk drawers for blank bumper stickers. I used to print my own slogans on them, things like RECYCLE OR DROWN IN GARBAGE. In my final campaign, I waged war against people who park illegally in handicapped spaces. I lurked in our supermarket parking lot hoping for a chance to use my I'M TOO LAZY TO WALK bumper sticker. When I saw a man jog into the store from the blue zone, I slapped one onto the back of his car. I didn't notice the geezer in the passenger seat until the man returned with a newspaper and unloaded a wheelchair from the back. Can you spell *mortification*?

This time I'll be more careful. While I print up a batch, I listen for Eva the Diva's return from cheerleading practice. The front door slams, and I follow the trail of sound—the refrigerator door sucking shut, the rustle of a plastic bag of tortilla chips, and the clang of a glass bowl on the kitchen counter. Eva's room door opens and closes. By the time I get there, it's locked.

"Lesbian Report," I announce in my loudest voice short of yelling.

She opens the door fast. "Do you want the whole neighborhood to hear?" she says.

The sight of Marshmallow curled prettily on her pillow irks me.

"So what's your deal messing me up onstage?" I ask. "I could tell Sapphire." But I won't, and she knows I won't. I push past her and shut the door behind me.

"If you're truly star material, Chub, nothing should faze you."

The skin in the middle of my back prickles, and I peel off my shirt. "Well, I'm not giving up the lead, if that's your plan."

"Doing a striptease for P. Tom?" she asks.

"Something's crawling on me."

Eva turns my shirt right side out and throws it at me. "Lesbian Report, huh? Just give it to me and get out."

I have her attention. "Okay," I say, thinking fast. "I had this freaky dream last night. I was looking for a cute guy to dance with at this party. But there were only girls around me—on the sofa, in the kitchen, on the porch. That's when I realized I was at a lesbian party."

"That's it?" Eva says. She straightens her gymnastics trophy.

"No," I say. "I felt really out of place at the party. Like I had a secret I couldn't tell anyone. After I woke up, it hit me. Lesbians who aren't out must feel that way at regular parties."

Eva looks like she wants to bean me with a trophy. I hope she doesn't use the volleyball league one because it's four feet tall. "You made that up, Chub. You think that if you pretend to be understanding, I'll tell you what you want to hear."

"Whatever," I say. "Next L Report item. I talked to Eyeliner Andie about your lesbian book."

"That pothead? You can't believe anything she says."

"She acted like she didn't know what I was talking about."

"Oh," Eva says. She pauses. "Maybe someone else lent me the book." She turns toward the barre. I meet her eyes in the mirror.

"There's a rumor that Andie is a lesbian," I say. "Do you think it's true?"

Eva's gaze slides away from mine. "How would I know?"

"Just tell me. Anything. I won't judge you. It's not like it matters if you're a lesbian. Or if she is. A lot of people choose that lifestyle."

"Lesbians don't *choose* to be lesbians," she says between her teeth.

"It's just an expression," I say. "You hear it all the time. A lifestyle choice blah, blah, blah."

"Just because you hear something, doesn't make it true. You don't get anything."

"Fill me in, then," I say.

"Even if I had something to tell, I wouldn't tell *you*." She counts off twelve deep pliés before continuing. "Remember that time with Elaine?"

"You mean in the fifth grade? I'd never, ever, ever do that now," I say.

"The lady doth protest too much, methinks," she says. Translation? One teensy mistake earns you a life sentence at Diva Penitentiary with no parole. Not even for family members.

Mom was all over me for my sloppy cursive that year. I didn't see the point of writing neatly. I could type already. So when I saw Eva copying her friend's homework paper,

I told on her. That way the parental disapproval would be distributed more fairly. *See, Mom? Eva's not perfect either.*

Anyway, Eva got in the last word. She spilled a full mug of cocoa on the diorama I'd left on the kitchen table. The next day, my math homework succumbed to spontaneous combustion. I apologized profusely to prevent further destruction and promised never to tattle again. She forgave me back then, so why bring up the whole thing now?

Marshmallow rubs her fuzzy cheek on Eva's knee. Traitor.

"If you won't talk to me because you don't trust me, that means you *are* a lesbian," I say. Sometimes I'm so clever it hurts.

"Ask Dad to cut off your tail tonight. It looks beyond stupid."

I pick up Marshmallow and gather myself to exit in a huff. Before I make it out the door, a change comes over her.

"Cheerleading practice is canceled tomorrow," she says. "You can give me the L Report after rehearsal. Meet you at the Silo."

There's a touch of spring thaw in the Ice Maiden's bosom after all. "Okay," I say.

Dad agrees to remove my beaver tail after dinner. The snug Bob Dylan T-shirt he has on reveals his most recent acquisition. A paunch. He seats himself on a crate on the back porch and positions me in front of him. The scissors feel cold against my neck. "So," he says, "what's the real story with your hair?"

"It's not a story. I cut it for a role," I say. "I'm playing a woman who pretends to be a man in the school play."

Dad continues snipping. "You look like a woman even with short hair," he says. "A beautiful young woman at that."

My throat tightens at this drop of honey, and my judgment falls victim to his sweetness.

"How would you feel," I say, "if one of your daughters grew up to be a lesbian?"

The snipping stops. Dad twirls me to face him, his eyes serious like the day he told us Grandma Peterson died. "Your mom and I have talked about it," he says, searching my face. "We said it wouldn't change anything. Of course, we'd be sad about no grandchildren."

"Lesbians have ovaries, Dad. Anyway, it was just a hypothetical question."

"Of course." He twirls me back and accidentally jabs my ear with the tip of the scissors.

Please don't Van Gogh me.

"Your mom wondered that time you asked for a tool set for your birthday," he says. "As if all that tractor driving she did in college wasn't just as suspicious."

I can feel hot blood rise up my neck. "That's so stereotypical," I say.

"True," he says. "But stereotypes often contain a grain of truth."

The phrase *not in this case* dances on my tongue. If I say it aloud, though, he might figure out that I mean Eva.

"Oops." Dad pulls back the scissors. "I cut your shirt by mistake."

"That's okay," I say. "It's stained anyway."

Elmo thinks he can handle having a lesbian daughter, but scissors speak louder than words. I thank him for the trim. Back in my room, I indulge in my latest secret pleasure, coming-out stories on the net. I read one by Cindy.

> Unlike many of you who post here, I was completely head over heels for boys at an early age. In high school alone, I had seven different boyfriends. None of them lasted long. I didn't think anything of it. Until I met Frieda my freshman year of college. It was the first time I felt that way about a girl, and she turned out to be my soul mate. We're still together three years later. I've never been happier.

She didn't notice she might like girls until she hit college? *I* am a bit of a tomboy. *I* asked for a tool set for my birthday. *I've* had five short-lived boyfriends. What if my obsession with boys turns out to be a repressed longing for girls?

Chapter 10

I slide *Better Than Chocolate* into my computer DVD player, engaging the English subtitles in case a certain someone has her ear pressed to my wall. I've never seen a girl kiss another girl, and imagining the act gives me an odd feeling, like when I picture Gethsemane and Elmo having sex. My legs jiggle while I wait for the first love scene. By the time it happens, I'm so into the story that the making-out part is neither gross nor earth-shattering. Normal. Ish.

A tap on the door gets me to click the stop button. Mom peeks in. "Lights out," she says. "You need your cutie rest." She smiles in a silly way.

"I'm already too cute."

"Go to bed or I'll reformat your hard drive."

"Okay, good night," I say.

When she's gone, I stuff an old towel in the crack under my door, lock it, and watch the rest of the movie, wondering if the "real thing" has ever taken place in the next room over.

I scoot into the school bike racks a few minutes after the bell. Fortunately, Mr. Beltz, who behaves as if a little whispering and note passing will cause the downfall of civilization, ignores tardiness. Go figure. With everyone safely dozing off in homeroom, I'm free to distribute my bumper stickers at will.

The bottom of Bryan's skateboard has an inviting blank spot. I peel off the backing and paste my sticker next to his PHANTOM, covering a bit of the skull and crossbones, but oh well. I read the result with satisfaction. SAVE THE GAYS! But will he appreciate the little details like the clip art showing two boys holding hands and the Web address I invented—www.YouLoseAgain.com?

I tag Carmen's bike next. Not nice, but just deserts for the divots she's made walking all over me with her spiky heels. Eva parks her car in the lot nearby. Should I tag her next? I waver. She asked me to give her the L Report at the Silo after school. That reminds me about the boxer shorts over the Barn door and how I need to take them down. But when I go to retrieve the ladder we use for aerial pranks, it's not there.

I circle to the front of the Barn. There's Jonathan coming down the ladder, the boxer shorts dangling from his back pocket. He smiles at me, his gorgeous eyes flashing friendliness. For a second, I wonder if I've entered a parallel universe where I'm someone he likes.

"You took them down?" I ask. "Hey, thanks."

He folds the ladder. "No big deal." Together we carry it to the storage spot. He hands me the boxers from his pocket. "I thought Aunt S asked you . . . you know, to convert me, or something."

If I were a cartoon character, a little balloon with a lightbulb inside would appear over my head. How Jonathan doesn't look like a typical juvenile delinquent, that he had to change schools, why he took down the insulting banner. I've been as oblivious as someone with an IQ in the single digits. Jonathan is gay. Then again, except for wearing dress shoes to school, he doesn't act like the gay men I've met—Dad's uncle and Mom's teaching assistant—nor the ones I've seen in movies. No eyeliner, no effusive hand gestures, no high-pitched giggle to tip me off.

"Convert you?" I ask. "Like convert you to straight? Sapphire wouldn't do that." I make the boxer shorts do a little dance. "I flirted with you because you're cute."

He grabs them back. "Let's burn them," he says.

"Okay," I say, thinking he's having me on.

He takes off into the field behind the Barn, and I follow him. The contents of his pack impress me—matches, newspaper, and bottle of rubbing alcohol. He wads the paper to make a little nest around the shorts.

"Are you a Boy Scout or something?" I ask.

"Aunt S says I'm a pyro."

He pours the alcohol and lights a match. Flames shoot up spectacularly, and then quickly burn out. We stomp the embers together. I've been initiated into "the club" after all.

"I never have any marshmallows when I need them," I say. His smile encourages me to continue. "Now someone can finally tell me Sapphire's real name."

He laughs out loud. "Sassafras? No? Sunshine? Don't believe me? How about Summer?"

"You're not going to tell me," I say.

He shakes his head. I don't know him well enough (yet) to tickle it out of him, so I drop it. For now.

When we make it back to the pavement, Jonathan wipes the dew off his shoes with a handkerchief. Okay, I can't picture Bryan doing that.

I duck into the bathroom to wash my hands. Haiku written in permanent marker decorates the wall by the mirror. Since we're near the English classrooms, some of it could be called literary—WHO'S AFRAID OF VAGINA WOOLF? and THOMAS HARDY GETS IT UP. A new addition reads RoZ iZ A CARPET MUNCHER. At first I don't get the joke, but the adjacent illustration explains everything. I add a line of my own—LESBIANS ARE THE BEST THESBIANS. Lame, I know, but I'm late for class.

Just as I reach my seat in homeroom, I notice Carmen's purse on it, a leather barricade with fashionable pockets. She who hesitates looks dumb. My walk practically oozes unconcern as I stroll over to a chair next to Eyeliner Andie. She touches the back of my head where my beavertail used to be.

"Better," she says.

Nico flashes me a micro smile before fixing his gaze on a fascinating poster about the water cycle.

"Carmen put up the boxer shorts," I say so she'll understand I'm not as clueless as I look.

"Now, that wasn't hard, was it?" she says.

Before lunch I duck into the bathroom to slather my eyes with indigo and bronze shadow. Bolstered by my exotic look, I head over to theater-geek central. I'll show Bryan how hot a dyke can be. When I round the corner, an unwelcome scene unfolds before me—Carmen stuffing a Frisbee up the front of his shirt. Tramp! *Fly-bitten flax-wench!* The one-sided fight she staged with Eva makes perfect sense now. She wanted to go after Bryan free and clear.

At this precise moment, Felicia's invitation to volunteer in the cafeteria kitchen seems like a good idea. When I get there, she doesn't notice me standing inches away from her trying not to slip on the treacherously wet floor. "Chef Roz reporting for duty," I say.

She opens a box of frozen pizzas. "You."

"At your service."

"You won't be cooking anything. Go help Anita with the vegetables." She points at a young woman by a steel counter.

Anita is young and playful, which makes the work more fun than I expected. I practice my Spanish on her, and she teaches me the words they don't cover in class. She compliments me on my eyeliner. Thirty minutes and one sliced finger later, I'm finished with my first shift. Felicia doesn't thank me when I leave.

After my last class, I go to the Barn for rehearsal. Since homeroom, Andie has added an iridescent green stripe to her eyeliner and folded over her pigtails so they point straight up from the top of her head. Not wanting to look like an inferior copy, I rush to the bathroom to remove my new eye makeup. Someone enters while I have my face in the sink. Luckily, that someone is only Sapphire.

"Why didn't you tell me about Jonathan?" I ask her.

She locks herself into a stall. "Tell you what about him?" *Tinkle tinkle.* I hate it when people hear me pee.

"That he's gay."

"He said that?" she says through the door.

"Yes." More or less.

The soap dispenser has been empty since my freshman year. Ditto the paper towel dispenser. I dry my face on the inside of my sweatshirt. I hear toilet paper unfurling and the toilet flushing. She emerges from the stall.

"Well, I'm not sure that he is," she says matter-of-factly. "Gay, I mean. The breakup with his girlfriend turned nasty. That could be the cause of his confusion."

She doesn't meet my eyes when she says this. For once I'm speechless. While she washes her hands, I stare. Adults are beyond comprehension, and she has become one of *them* for the first time since I've known her. She blows on her hands to dry them. I don't think to offer her my sweatshirt. We return to the stage without further conversation.

In today's scene, Nico plays the pitiful shepherd, Silvius, rejected by the woman he loves, Carmen/Phebe. Nico's performance reminds me of the radio ads produced in Yolo Bluffs:

"Oh, no, Susie! It's only three days till Christmas, and I haven't bought any presents."

"I know, let's go to Annie's Home Gifts. They have something for the whole family. Toys for the kids, a tea cozy for Aunt Betty, and an electric meat fork for Dad."

"Great! Let's go right now."

After the first unsuccessful run-through, Sapphire attacks Nico with a bottle of styling mousse and a comb. He's more attractive with a forehead. The new vulnerability doesn't change the stiffness of his performance, though. Between scenes Carmen hangs on to him and whispers in his ear like he's a finalist for *Teen Idol. Whey-faced flirt-gill.* She ate Bryan for lunch and is having Nico for a snack—so who did she devour for breakfast? She used to be such a prude. Never even had a boyfriend.

Sapphire finally calls for a break, and Eva offers me something to eat—sliced peppers with ranch dressing. When I bite down, a crazy burning sensation starts with my lips and travels along my tongue, lighting my throat on fire. I do an immediate flip across the hardwood floor followed by extreme hopping and shrieking for water. Carmen pours a bottle of Evian over my head.

"It's not my hair, stupid, it's my mouth!" I shout. At which point she sloshes water in my face and down my front.

"I'm so sorry," Eva says. "I didn't know they were spicy."

There's never a lie detector around when you need one. Not that I need one. I know this is another one of her ploys to undermine my performance. Even after downing a bucket of water, I can barely talk. Sapphire asks Carmen to take over my role since she knows all my lines. I watch the action from a place off to the side, glowering all the while until Bryan joins me. I try to bring my nervous mannerisms under control for his benefit.

"How's it going with your dad's girlfriend?" I ask, stuffing my fingertips into my pockets.

"Not good. She's a total clean freak," he says. "She called me a moron when I accidentally got some grease on her new kitchen towels."

"Harsh," I say. My metal chair clunks as I stand up.

"I'll survive."

We watch Nico struggle through his lines one more time.

"Do I ever sound that bad?" Bryan says.

"Oh, please. You're magnificent."

He turns toward me. "No. That shirt is magnificent," he says.

I look down. My bright pink bra shows through the wet cloth. My brain turns to Jell-O, the ridiculous kind with embedded fruit cocktail and mini marshmallows.

"I don't believe in pink," I say. Onstage, Carmen delivers my next line with finesse. I take some consolation that while she's usurping my starring role with Eva's help, I'm usurping Eva's perfect boyfriend. Yon Bryan has a lean and hungry look. Translation? Who am I to resist? I kiss him on the lips.

Chapter 11

The second our lips touch, impulse control kicks in for once. I back away.

"Don't stop." He drags me behind the speaker. "I'll make you forget your grrlfriend."

Oh, I get it now. Fury takes over from confusion. I'm a test of his virility. He's thinking, "One kiss from a sexy scoundrel like me and *poof* she's hetero again." I make to slap him, and he grabs my wrists. He has to let go when my knee threatens his prize possessions. The course of true love never did run smooth. Translation? The difference between a prince and a toad is overrated because they are both just boys underneath the glitter and the warts.

I exit without a backward glance, buttoning my lace-edged cardigan over my wet shirt. Did Eva see our little kiss? I'll find out soon enough if she keeps our date at the Silo. I zoom toward town on my scooter, and the cold air clears my head. While I wait for my espresso at a little table in the café, I text Eva to gauge her mood. I need to be prepared.

"Darest thou show thy vllns face?" I write. Shakespearean language is murder on the fingers. When my shot arrives, I doctor it with generous amounts of milk and sugar. Mom says caffeine will stunt your growth. Too bad she didn't tell me that before my growth spurt.

Eva's reply: **"I hsten frthwth 2 yor side."**

So she didn't see me kiss Bryan. I still have the high moral ground in our little war, and I plan to press my advantage. When she arrives and settles in next to me with her decaf chai, I stare her down without saying a word. This technique encourages confession according to several psychology Web sites. Ten minutes from now, she'll be prostrate on the floor apologizing for poisoning me at rehearsal.

"Don't be like that," she says. "You're not usually wimpy about a little spice."

"So you admit it," I say. "Did Carmen put you up to it?"

"Just give me the L Report," she whispers. "And quietly."

The café is deserted except for a middle-aged man with a comb-over and the barista, whose bored expression says that she could care less whether we're discussing the life cycle of ferns or the Kama Sutra. Besides, no one even knows what the *L* stands for except us. I'm about to shout "Lesbian Report" when I notice Eva sitting on the edge of her seat folding and unfolding her napkin. I lower my sword. What's done is done. Translation? I suffer from adoration-induced amnesia. Chili peppers, what chili peppers?

"What do you want to know?" I say quietly.

"Anything. What happened at school today."

"Okay," I say. "When I came into the locker room, Jada had her top off. You know that uptight girl on student council? My locker happens to be close to hers. When I walked past, she covered her chest with her T-shirt."

"Details," Eva says. She rests her hand on my arm. It feels good, like when Mom used to drape a sheet over the kitchen table and we would crawl under pretending to be prairie dog sisters in the dim light.

I ham it up. "Her eyes got all huge. She acted like I might grab her breasts and ravish her. *Boil-brained simp*."

Eva's look says sympathy and disgust, with a little fascination sprinkled on top.

"I mean, her chest is as flat as a soccer field," I add.

"So what'd you do?"

"I told her the truth. Her boobs were nothing to look at. I've seen mosquito bites bigger."

Eva laughs so hard that she chokes on her chai. "You're a riot."

Actually, this whole incident barely happened, and I didn't say anything at all to Jada. But what's a little vacation from reality if I can make Eva laugh?

"There's more," I say. "Jonathan's one of us."

"You mean . . . ?" she asks in a breathy voice, one hand fluttering over her heart. "A long-lost Peterson? I always wanted a brother."

"No," I say, but I'm laughing too. "He's gay."

"He told you that?"

"Pretty much. And he took down the boxer shorts over the Barn for me." I skip the part about the bonfire.

"Cool." She brings her creased napkin to her lips.

The door opens, and I look up. Eyeliner Andie and Nico enter holding hands.

Eva stands. "Well, I'm off," she says. She and Andie nod at each other as they pass.

Andie sits down next to me. "Why did you leave rehearsal early?" she asks.

Nico stops hovering, sits down too, and picks at an unidentifiable glob on the table with his nail. "Because of my sorry acting," he says. With the mousse still in his hair, I can see his eyes up close for once. His eyelids droop downward in an attractive curve.

"Your acting is fine," I say. No point in lowering his morale now that he's been cast as Silvius. The minute the playbill is posted, we theater geeks become a team.

He laughs through his nose and makes eye contact with the table. What an unlikely couple they are. Eyeliner Andie lights up the room like a neon sign when she talks, while Nico flickers on and off—her fifteen-watt sidekick. Her nails are painted denim blue with gold zippers down the center. Obviously my problem is boring nail polish.

"Did you know that Nico's from Mexico?" Andie asks.

"You don't have an accent."

"I don't believe in accents," he says in an Antonio Banderas accent. "Besides, I moved here before I could talk." He tells this to the sugar dispenser.

"His mom is Mayan," Andie says. She sounds like a used car salesman selling her used boyfriend. Notice the antilock brakes and rear suspension. Maybe she read my mind, heard my unkind thoughts about him. My knee jostles my tote and tips it over. The famous lesbian novel, *Annie on My Mind,* falls out. I had wedged it in at the top of my bag to pique Eva's curiosity.

Eyeliner Andie picks it up off the floor. "Do you like it?" she asks.

"It's good. A little old-fashioned."

"Classics are fine, but I've got something more current." She opens her green poodle purse with buttons all over it and takes out a book called *Boy Meets Boy*. "Way cool. And funny too." Her lovely Egyptian eyes bore into me. "There's a lot more where that came from. My bedroom's practically a library. You should check it out sometime."

She's coming on to me. In a single, graceless motion, I knock my coffee onto the floor with my forearm. The barista gives me a look that says "They don't pay me enough to mop up after a clumsy ditz like you."

"I don't believe in coffee." I throw a pile of brown napkins on the puddle.

Nico collects the soggy heap to deposit into the trash. While he's across the room, Andie whispers into my ear. "Can you give Nico pointers on acting when you come over?"

Oh. She didn't want to compromise my virginity. She wanted acting lessons for Nico.

"Why wait?" I say. Nico comes back to the table. "We are going to do a little acting practice."

"Good idea." He looks at me at last. His irises are chocolaty brown.

"Let's start with body language. I'll act Carmen. Since I can't do that hair-nibbling thing, I'll do her posture." I stand up. "Ever notice how she throws back her shoulders?" I thrust out my chest and strut like a Flamenco dancer.

"That's so totally her!" Andie says.

I sultrify my voice. "Oh, Nico, you said your lines so beautifully."

Nico flushes. Pink looks good on his dark cheeks.

"Why don't you say your first lines as Silvius? Be Silvius in love with Carmen, the shepherdess who won't give you the time of day."

He drones dutifully, "Sweet Phebe, do not scorn me; do not, Phebe! Say that you love me not, but say not so in bitterness. The common executioner, whose heart—"

I cut him off. "You sound like a corpse."

"I'm not into Carmen," he snaps.

"Despite what the tabloids say, actors who perform love scenes together aren't usually in love with each other. Imagine you're wooing Andie instead."

Nico looks at his watch. "I have to go. I told someone . . . I promised my . . . Later." He launches himself out of the Silo without turning back. Eyeliner Andie chases after him.

"Is it something I said?" I yell.

"I'll call you tonight," she says before dashing out.

While scooting home in the twilight, I obsess over the details of my afternoon with the mysterious Andie, from the color of her lip liner to how she looked at me when I talked to her. I could write a different book—*Andie on My Mind*.

When I get home, everyone is already seated at the dinner table. Eva gives me the evil eye. What now? Did she call Jada to verify my locker-room story?

Dad brings out his signature dish—split pea soup. I ladle myself a bowlful, discarding the chunks of former pig butt that float to the top. I don't bother being discreet about this. Elmo's mini freak-out over my hypothetical lesbianhood has made me a touch peevish toward him. I don't like the way he's been looking at me lately, either.

"Sorry. I forgot," he says to me.

"That's okay. I'll feed the ham bits to Marshmallow," I say.

"How did rehearsal go?" Mom asks Eva.

"Fine. The usual," she says.

If the parents knew one tenth of what goes on beneath the surface of our lives, they'd be riveted. We're quality programming. Time to turn up the heat on our lukewarm dinner conversation.

"Not fine," I say. "I couldn't talk after Eva tricked me into eating a red-hot chili pepper."

This gets Mom's attention. "That doesn't sound like Eva."

"I told you it was an accident," Eva says. There are daggers in her smile pointed at my heart. Translation? Two can play the Shock the Parents game. I brace myself. "Carmen called. . . ."

Uh-oh. This has to be about my SAVE THE GAYS! bumper sticker. But I'm not the kind of girl who lets herself be done to death by a slanderous tongue without a fight.

"Carmen called? I thought you weren't talking," I say.

My ploy works. Gethsemane switches to her patented overreaction mode. "You still aren't talking?" she asks.

"It's only been a few days, Mom," Eva says. "Something must be going on at home because she quit cheerleading."

"Did she tell you why?" Mom asks.

"No." Eva frowns. She tosses out the next words like a fast series of needle-sharp darts. "She told me she saw Roz with Bryan at rehearsal."

I'm in trouble in so many ways I can't keep track. I turn

to Dad to change the subject. "Did Janis take a vacation?" I ask him.

"Janis?"

I point to his plain green T-shirt. "Janis Joplin. Isn't that her shirt?" My desperate joke generates zero laughter and provides only the briefest of diversions.

"She saw you kiss him," Eva says.

"Did not!"

"No catfights at the dinner table. They spoil my appetite," Dad says.

"Roz, did you?" Mom says.

"I've never chased after Eva's boyfriends."

"Except John and Marcus," Eva says.

Dad takes his bowl into the kitchen.

"Those were *ex*-boyfriends. Anyway, Carmen's full of cra—crabmeat." I'm lying, of course, but only a little, since I regretted kissing Bryan afterward. "Carmen's after him herself. She stuffed a Frisbee up his shirt at lunch."

Mom looks bewildered. She couldn't be more confused than if a new scientific study proved that broccoli causes cancer. Eva stares at me in disbelief, and then laughs so hard, soup sprays from her mouth.

"What's so funny?" I ask.

"Carmen absolutely detests Bryan."

"What?" Open your eyes, sister.

I finish my soup while Eva persists in her delusions. "When I got together with Bryan," she says, "Carmen didn't talk to me for two weeks."

"It was hard for her because she didn't have a boyfriend," Mom says.

"Or maybe she wanted Bryan for herself," I say.

Mom kicks me under the table.

After dinner Eva readies herself for miniature golf while I clean up the kitchen, my punishment for refusing to go. I run water into the empty soup pot. I do remember Carmen icing out Bryan when he linked up with Eva. New boyfriends have a way of dominating a girl's time, a thing a best friend can resent. The front door closes. I leave the pot to soak overnight and go online. Andie is connected. Here's my chance to ask her directly if she's crushing on me.

Me: want 2 play mini golf 2nite?

Andie: only if i can kill myself 1st *checks drano supply*

Me: never mind

Me: what happened at the silo 2day?

Andie: a lot

Me: do u like nico?

Andie: like or like like?

Me: like like

Andie: hmmm

Me: does he like like u?

Andie: maybe

This is going nowhere.

Me: there's a rumor that u r a lesbian

Andie: lesbian schlesbian i hate labels *gnashes teeth*

Andie: i fall in love with who i fall in love with

Me: so u r bisexual?

Andie:

Me: so u like girls sometimes, I mean

Andie: doesn't every1?

Me: i mean like like

Andie: who do u like like?

Me: i dunno

Andie: rehearse with me at Nico's 2moro? I'll get u at 10

Me: ok

Andie: ttyl

I'm a chicken. A confused chicken. The conversation leaves me wondering about labels, though, and why Andie hates them so much. After all, labels help you figure out how to behave. Like, say you're on a date with a brainy dude. You're more likely to impress him if you mention an article from *Wired* than one from *Cosmo*. Or if you're a girl attracted to girls—aka a lesbian—you don't waste your time and heart crushing on a straight girl. Then again, I don't like being labeled as Eva's big-boned, less-talented little sister.

I log on to a gay teen Web site to learn more about

categories and chase down a link to Alfred Kinsey, a sexologist in the 1950s. Yes, they had sex back then, despite the goofy clothes. He's dead now, but in his warm-blooded days he researched sexuality. He wrote that sexual orientation is a continuum. He even created a scale for people to rate themselves: 0 = exclusively heterosexual, 1–5 = the gray area in between, 6 = exclusively homosexual. Who knew there was such a big gray area?

I know I'm not a 6, but who says I couldn't be a 1?

Chapter 12

After a night of patchy sleep, my eyelids feel as squishy as overripe apricots. I should ease up on the late-night self-questioning. Though I've already lost four pounds on my new diet, hauling my body out of bed reminds me of wrestling bags of compost from the pickup last spring for Mom's garden. Eyeliner Andie will be here in an hour.

I spend the entire morning mismatching accessories in a vain attempt to develop a funky new look. I shouldn't have bothered. Andie arrives at my door wearing a fake fur hat and snaky black eyeliner—Cleopatra goes Cossack. Does my heart beat a little faster when she arrives? Her boots have stiletto heels that wobble when she walks.

"A car, a car, my kingdom for a car," she says.

"It's only two blocks from here," I say. Our progress is slow. Andie takes off her boots for the last half block. Nico's house is a dusty blue color with cobwebs on the window screens, fronted by dull grass and one small olive tree. It has an erased look, except for the bright green front door with mysterious symbols painted onto each of the six panels. I've never been inside before. I knock.

Nico opens the door right away, and as I slide by him into the house, I estimate that I outweigh him by several pounds. The seating arrangement in the living room is original—two chairs shaped like hands surrounded by floor pillows. A basket of rocks and bones (animal bones, I hope) sits next to an umbrella stand.

Nico takes us into the kitchen to meet his grandma. She scowls at Andie and me from under her visor cap before offering us mugs of hot chocolate. Nico sprinkles his with spices from a small wooden bowl. I do the same. The flavors battle on my tongue, but my good upbringing makes me take a second sip.

"Delicious," I say.

"And you think you're such a great actress," Andie scoffs.

"Thank you," I say to Nico's grandma.

"I'm going out," she mutters. "Behave."

Nico collapses into a hand chair while Andie and I sit together on the big pillows. "You two look good like that," he says. Or is this his flirty twin brother?

Andie smooshes her cheek against mine. My heart clangs in my chest like a clumsy thief in a dark garage. Andie like likes me. Imagining a crush on Andie in the privacy of my mind is totally different from having a real girlfriend with real hands and real lips. I do the reasonable thing—hide my panic with efficient action.

"Let's get to work," I say.

Oblivious to my mini freak-out, Andie extracts a small pipe from her bag. "May I?" she asks. "I can concentrate better when I'm high."

"Pot messes with your memory," I say. "Once my

ex-boyfriend went onstage stoned. He said his lines okay. Sadly, they were lines from a different play."

"That was Marcus, right?" Andie says. "I thought he was Eva's ex." She holds a lighter to the bowl and inhales. After a few seconds, she exhales through the open window.

"Put that away," I say in my tyrant voice.

Andie hurls a loose pillow at my chest.

"Pillow fight," Nico yells. He charges, whacking me over the head.

"Get him," Andie says. I body-slam him with my floor pillow while she pummels him from behind.

Nico knocks me over. "Bombs away," he shrieks.

I bump into the porcelain umbrella stand. It topples. When Nico rights it, I see that a wedge of pottery has chipped off the rim. This is the fourth time I've broken something in less than a month. Sierra would be able to explain it. I'll have to email her with the whole crazy story.

"Grandma will kill me." He fetches a bottle of glue to reattach the shard. "Fight's over," he says when he finishes the repair. "Time to kiss and make up. Ladies first."

Andie puts her hands on the back of my neck and pulls my face toward hers.

NOT. But would I kiss her back if she did?

When Nico says, "Time to kiss and make up. Ladies first," Andie laughs so hard she can barely stay upright.

"So that's your perverted plan," she gasps between giggles. "Sorry. No free show for Nico. Roz is cute, but she's not exactly my type. Don't think *you're* getting any kisses either."

Her rejection hurts my shallow ego. "What's your type?" I ask.

"More toward the Goth."

I slip into a bad German accent to cover my feelings. "Thiss iss a sserious rehearssal. Makink out iss abssolutely verboten. Infractionss vill be punisht by floggink."

Nico shakes his hair over his eyes. Good-bye, flirtatious Nico; hello, sullen Nico.

"Let's go powder our noses." Andie drags me down the hall, pushes me into a room, and shuts the door.

I look at the messy bed, dirty clothes draped on a chair, and dresser drawers not quite closed. "Why did you bring me into Nico's room?" I say.

"To show you something." She points to a group of candid photos tacked to the bottom of a poster from our last school play. They're all of me. "Nico likes you. Like likes."

"So he's really into lesbians?" I say. Is this a test?

"Maybe." Her lips curve into that Mona Lisa smile of hers. She follows it with an exaggerated wink that wrecks the effect. We go back to the living room.

Nico positions the umbrella stand with the damaged side toward the wall. Andie puts away her pipe and plays Phebe in Nico's scene, scorning him most passionately. Nico says his lines with two emotions—forced anger and fake enthusiasm. I coach him on voice control, body language, and the scenery of the mind. After that he's slightly better than terrible.

When Andie woos me in the second half of the scene, I freak out again because I kind of like it, which means maybe I'm falling for her. But at the end of the scene, she hugs herself and rolls around on the floor making kissy noises. "But I love myself best of all," she says.

"New scene," I say. While Andie is still in full hysteria mode, Nico's grandma returns from her errand and fixes her piercing scowl on the umbrella stand.

"Maybe you should go," Nico mumbles.

We gather our things in silence and hurry outside. The slippery leaves on the brick walk squish under my shoes. I fan myself with my script.

"Want to go somewhere and smoke?"

"Pot gives me a headache," I say primly.

"Come anyway. I'd love the company."

"I have to reorganize my closet," I say. She said I wasn't her type, and though one part of me feels relieved, the other part of me feels hurt. Okay, I admit it. Girls aren't a lot easier to understand than boys, after all.

By nightfall I've forgiven Andie for rejecting me. It's not her fault that I'm as un-Goth as Mary Poppins. I have to learn to accept the way things are. Andie and Nico go around like a couple. Andie likes me. Maybe Nico like likes me, while I don't know how I feel about either of them in the romantic sense. But I wish I could redo the scene on the sidewalk outside Nico's house when Andie asked me to hang out. She's my closest friend at the moment, though I barely know her. How pathetic is that? She's online, so I IM her.

Me: hey, sorry bout 2day *slinks with tail between legs*

Me: i was feeling bitchy

Andie: no big

Me: thnx *pops a bottle of bubbly*

Me: i think carmen is just pretending

Me: she doesn't really like like nico

Andie: no duh

Me: she's covering for her tete a tetes with bryan

Andie: not

Me: then y pretend? *bites pinkie nail in confusion*

Andie: u r a smart girl

Andie: u figure it out

Me: y do u know so much?

Andie: i observe people, i notice things

Me: aren't u speshul

With a friend like Andie, who needs adventure? Prozac could come in handy, though. After signing off, I send the world's longest email to Sierra. In it, I confess all that I've done and cross my fingers that she won't take a month to answer back.

Chapter 13

On Sunday afternoon when Eva returns from her piano recital, I dangle a salacious Lesbian Report as an incentive for her to drive me to the outlet mall. She agrees without hesitation. Soon enough I figure out why. The inside of her car acts as the perfect soundproof bubble. She chews me out the second I slam my door closed.

"You think rehearsals are bad now? If you don't leave Bryan alone, it's going to get worse." Rant. Rant. Rant.

"I'm no threat," I say. "I'm a dyke, remember?"

She ignores this, punctuating her long tirade with abrupt and unnecessary stomps on the gas pedal. The crazy accelerations make the point rather effectively. I'm guessing that lesbians aren't usually this touchy about their boyfriends. My theory about Eva's sexual orientation—thin and shaky to begin with—enters its final death throes and expires on the threadbare carpet at my feet.

While we're stopped at a light, she wipes the inside of the windshield with a small towel because the fan broke two years ago. I slide a Good Charlotte tape into the player and turn the volume on high. Her ancient Honda doesn't do CDs. I meant to spin an exciting version of events at Nico's house yesterday, but her venting has put me in a dark mood.

When she pulls into the parking lot, the tires screech. "What happened to the L Report, Ch—Roz?"

I could mention her hateful lecturing, but she stopped herself just before using my hated nickname, and that act of grace softens my resolve to fight with her. Besides, I need someone to talk to. Maybe Eva can break Andie's secret code.

"Why do you think Carmen's all over Nico like cat hair on velvet?" I say.

"He's kind of cute in a depressed, punky way."

"I guess," I say. "Andie and I went to Nico's house yesterday for acting lessons."

"And he taught you some advanced techniques," she says.

"Ha ha. I was hoping to loosen him up a little. While we were practicing, Andie acted like she might kiss me."

"In front of Nico?" Eva lowers her voice. Sitting in the car with her—the windows clouded with the moisture from our breaths—I get that under-the-kitchen-table feeling again.

"Details," Eva says.

"We were doing the scene where Phebe falls for Rosalind. Andie looked at me with burning lust. Maybe it was the pot talking."

"What will you do if she does? Kiss you, I mean."

"Kiss her back."

Eva squeezes the steering wheel with both hands, I'm guessing to keep herself from strangling me. "I get it. You're so engrossed in the *role,* you think you're a lesbian now."

Why do I do that? I should carry around a pair of socks to stuff in my mouth whenever I get the urge to stir things up. Clean and sassy socks. With lace cuffs. Still, I'd like to know what she thinks of Kinsey's ideas.

"Pretend the dashboard is a line," I say. "The far left equals lesbian and the far right equals heterosexual. Everything in between is bisexual, okay?"

"If you say so," she says, her eyes still focused on the opaque windshield.

"I'm about here," I say, pointing to the glove compartment door. "If Ms. Perfect came along, I could fall in love with her." Maybe.

"So you're in love with Andie." She drops the steering wheel and flexes her fingers.

"Not exactly. I'm just curious."

Eva turns toward me. "Have you ever dreamed about making out with a girl?"

"No. But I dreamed that I kissed that fat, ugly guy with the bumpy nose at Pet Mania—"

"And you woke up screaming." She cracks a smile.

We're having a bonding moment. Then I go and ruin it. "How about you? Any hot girl-on-girl dreams?"

"Will you stop with that, Chub?" She snatches up her bag off the backseat. "Let's go in."

While Eva the Diva searches through the size threes, I suppress the urge to suffocate her with an XL jog bra. Why did I inherit the Amazon genes? I remind myself that she can't help being Tinker Bell. "I'll tell you a secret if you tell me one."

"I don't have any secrets."

"None that you'll tell me," I say.

She holds up a pair of pants with embroidery at the hem. "These would look good on you. See if they have your size." She's like one of those amazing rope knots with no beginning and no end, no obvious spot to start unraveling.

"I didn't finish the Lesbian Report."

She darts a look at the people around us. "Let's go try these on," she says.

We take adjacent changing rooms. "No one knows us here," I say. "We could liven up their dull lives by having a real conversation."

"Shut up." She launches a plastic hanger over the barrier with painful accuracy.

"Ow. What can we talk about, then?"

"How those pants fit."

Back in our soundproof car bubble, she revs the engine and drops the clutch into reverse. Grinding gears smell sweet and smoky. "I'm a private person," she says. "I don't even like to talk about what I ate for lunch in front of strangers."

"Okay, okay. You want to hear the rest?" The fog has thickened. We crawl along at tortoise speed because this freeway is known for its multiple-car accidents. "Andie told me she falls in love with who she falls in love with. Does that sound the same as bisexual?"

"More like confused."

"I thought you two were friends."

"In your mind, Chub."

I scan the local radio stations for something to fill the silence and settle on a mushy oldie.

"I used to love that song," Eva says, turning up the volume. "I played it like twenty times that day I canceled my birthday party. Was that fifth or sixth grade?"

"Fifth for me, sixth for you." The taillights of the car ahead appear and disappear in the fog.

"None of my friends could come, remember? You said they were all losers and I was perfect. I hated that you said that."

Back then, she was my goddess and I her disciple. I once pretended to *be* her for a week, dressed exclusively in leotards and ballet shoes until Mom made me stop.

"You hated that I thought you were perfect?"

She rolls her eyes.

"Don't worry," I add. "I don't think you're perfect anymore."

"Hooray!"

"Hooray what?"

"I can barely see the road." She wipes the windshield again. "Maybe I need glasses."

I reach over and remove her sunglasses.

Five songs later, we arrive home. "I thank thee for thy gracious transport," I say.

Monday morning after fortifying myself with a banana and a spoonful of almond butter, I leave the house. Suddenly an army of girls in baggy sweatshirts and short spiky hair mobs me. *We love you, Roz.* They crash and grind like crazed metal fans.

And I have a bunny who does my homework in exchange for ear massages. NOT.

Picture this—moldy peach flesh smeared across the

shiny chrome of my scooter. And scrawled in black on the body: DYKEBYKE. That *swag-bellied measle*! Except Carmen doesn't have an extra ounce of fat on her. I spit on the word and scrub at it with my palm, but the homophobic twit used permanent marker. At that moment, I decide to follow her around for the day. It could prove educational.

I throw my besmirched scooter through my bedroom window and change from frilly frippery into gray sweats, which are better for spying. After hiding my scooter under my bed, I cruise to school on foot. When I reach the bike racks, I notice that the paint on Carmen's bike has been scraped to the metal where my SAVE THE GAYS! bumper sticker used to be. Oh, that.

When I enter homeroom, Carmen sits up straight and throws every bit of skill she has into ignoring me. Despite her flirty pink crop top and fur-lined clogs, she looks forlorn sitting by herself. She had a fight with her best friend, dropped out of cheerleading, barely got the third-best part in the play, and then some quasi-lesbo delinquent tagged her bike. I shake off the sympathy moment. It's not like she's Mother Teresa either.

I slip a note to Eyeliner Andie after I'm settled.

wouldn't u like it if someone thot u were perfect?

She pretends to strangle herself with her ring-covered fingers.

what a burden! i want to be loved for who i am.

But did Marilyn Monroe expect to be loved for who she was? How about Madonna? They invented themselves and became international icons. Settling for your plain old self lacks ambition. If everyone loves you for who you are, why improve? Then again, Madonna's kind of creepy (in a fun way), and Marilyn killed herself.

Nico slides into his seat and reads the note. His hair twitches as he writes, so I can tell he's blinking. He flicks the paper my way.

i AM perfect.

During gym I pseudo-sprain my ankle on the basketball court, cursing under my breath and hopping on one foot so sincerely that the coach sends me to the school nurse. Free at last to spy on Carmen, I ensconce myself in the empty bathroom she usually primps in before lunch. Before entering the center stall, I grimace at my reflection in the mirror. Am I sinking too low?

Someone comes in. From under the partition I see that she has very large feet in boyish loafers. I wisely stand on the toilet seat. Just what I need is another rumor about me. Did you know that RoZ iZ constipated? When the bell rings, Bigfoot goes into a stall. A half dozen other girls pile in and stand in front of the mirror.

Carmen: My lip gloss has disappeared again.
Carmen Groupie I: Use mine. God, I wish I could get my hair to grow like yours.
Groupie II: Is it true you dropped out of cheerleading?
Groupie I: I heard you had a fight with Eva.
Carmen: Eva who?

As one actress evaluating another of lesser talent, her words sound forced.

Groupie II: Eva's so stuck up.

I restrain myself from bursting from the stall and smacking groupie II.

Groupie I: Who are the beautiful lips for?
Carmen: Someone else's boyfriend.
Groupies I and II, in unison: Oooooooh!

No matter what Andie says, that girl is SO after Bryan. I offer a prayer to the goddess of spy-chick luck. If I can catch them alone together, Eva will have to admit she was wrong. When the bathroom clears out, I flush the toilet. That wastes water, I know, but social convention demands it. Bigfoot and I exit at the same time. Only she's not a girl. She's Jonathan.

Chapter 14

I *grab Jonathan's arm* and drag him out of the bathroom. Our hasty exit unfortunately doesn't escape notice. A boy from my English class—a wrestling team–type dude—veers from his path to bother us.

"What's up, girly-man?" MuscleBound says. He sniggers at his own dull wit.

"Get out of my way, you *gorbellied clotpole,*" I say.

"What did you just call me, lawn mower?"

"At least I don't have a dick in the middle of my face like you," I say.

The mood turns ugly. I clench my fists ready to fight. It's Jonathan's turn to drag me.

"Let's go," he says.

"Sissies," MuscleBound yells after us.

Jonathan tightens his grip so I can't turn back to deck his sorry butt. BlueDragon joins our escape. A strand of yellow construction-site tape clings to his fur and trails behind him as he walks. We make an awesome threesome. A good distance from campus we slow down.

"Sissy," I say to Jonathan. We both laugh hard at this, but he gets serious again.

"Aunt S would kill me if I got into another fistfight," he says.

"Is that why you left your school in Bakersfield?"

"More or less," he says. "What *did* you call that guy?"

I recognize the ploy—asking a question to evade answering another question—because I use it all the time. He'll tell me when he's ready. "I called him a fat dummy."

He flashes me a genuinely happy smile, and I feel good. The morning fog has burned off, revealing naked blue sky in all directions.

"What were you doing in the girls' bathroom?" I ask.

"Freshening my makeup," he says. I can see by the curve of his lips he's having me on. "Where to?" he adds.

I'm so glad he wants to hang out with me, I don't care that he evaded another question. *Pariah* might be too strong of a word, but lately I get more brooding stares than friendly hugs. I debate where to take him. The Silo is too public, and the benches at Yolo Park are usually sticky from spilled toddler snacks. "Follow me." I lead the way up a trail to the reservoir overlook. "Did you hear what Carmen said in the bathroom?" I ask as we climb upward.

"Yeah. So?" he says.

"So she's way worse than a *gorbellied clotpole*."

"Hmmm," he says.

By that I gather he doesn't agree. "You don't know her as well as I do," I say. If I'm the serpent under the flower, she's the Hydra—a nine-headed snake—under the swamp. He'll find out soon enough. When we reach the top and catch our breath, I gesture grandly to the view below. "Are not these woods more free from peril than the envious court?"

Jonathan hugs himself against the cold. "But here we feel the churlish chiding of the winter's wind, which bites and blows." Translation? Jonathan thinks I'm a heartless gossip. Where's my stylish mouth gag when I need it? Then again, maybe he's just cold. The gusts make waves across the silvery water surface of the reservoir. We flop over on a stone bench against a small cliff that offers some protection from the elements. BlueDragon rests his weight against me and goes to sleep.

"Your voice is made for Shakespeare," I say.

He snorts. "Shakespeare is a white dude's dude."

"Othello is black." I flick his new earring, a gold hoop.

"And a murderer." He props himself up against a boulder and stretches out his legs like he owns the place. His easy smile gives me the courage to be bold.

"Sapphire told me you had a girlfriend," I say. "Was that weird? I mean being with a girl when you're gay?"

"Girls are okay. I go both ways, I guess."

"That's how I am too," I say, venturing slightly off the path of reality.

"No shit." He looks at me with interest.

"No shit. I don't like limiting my options to half the population." When said aloud, it sounds like one of my better ideas, to be honest.

He takes my hand in his and holds it in a friendly way. A delicious feeling comes over me. Normally holding hands causes more anxiety than bliss. Are my teeth clean? Are my lips chapped? But Jonathan isn't giving me the kissing vibe. The only flaw is the lie that I'm living. It's like when you spill soda on your new white tank top, just a drop, but it lands right next to your nipple, so everyone can't help but notice it. Maybe I should tell him the truth. I shiver at the thought.

"You cold, Broadway? Let's make a fire."

"Sounds nice. But if you have to call me names, can you at least pick something cute? Broadway makes me sound fat."

"I'm all over it, Short Stuff."

"Thanks a bunch, Pyro."

"Don't mention it, Pee Wee."

When I've gathered a pile of sticks, Jonathan pours yellow powder from a container of nondairy creamer into a paper cup.

"What else do you have in that mystery pack?" I say, admiring his weirdness.

"This stuff burns like crazy," he says. When he lights a match, the powder bursts into flame and the dry wood catches. He looks like a proud kid. I stretch my hands over the fire to show my appreciation.

"Have you ever had a boyfriend?" I ask.

"Have you ever had a girlfriend?"

"No. But I made one up to impress my friends," I say.

"Me, not even that." He spreads his fingers and looks at me through the gaps. "But I daydream about my brother's best friend."

"Maybe he likes you back," I say.

He holds his hands over the fire next to mine. I can almost see through his pale palms to the bones beneath. His face reads pained, like when Dad talks about his failed college grunge band. "No chance. He's pure hetero."

A small beetle trundles up his pant leg. I pick it off and

set it on his arm. We watch as it negotiates his sweater's nubby terrain.

"Did you always know about yourself?" I ask.

"Pretty much. How about you?"

"No, but I'm easily confused." The beetle reaches his hand and cruises across his smooth skin. We're friends, and it feels good. Since he's new at school, I don't have to share him with anyone else, either.

"I'm glad you moved here." Immediately I see that I said the wrong thing again. "Hit me. I'm a jerk," I add.

A flock of geese in arrow formation passes overhead. He looks wary now, like Marshmallow when she has a bird in her mouth. "You're not a jerk," he says.

"If you ever want to talk about it. . . ." But why would he tell me? I'm the gossip geek of Yolo Bluffs, the Typhoid Mary of secrets.

He shakes off the beetle into the fire.

I punch him hard in the arm. "Why did you do that?"

"What?" he says, all innocent. "What'd I do?"

When I enter the Barn for rehearsal, Carmen's all cozied up to Nico, sitting on the stage with her legs dangling over the edge. Eva and Bryan are in a private corner reviewing a script. I flop down next to Carmen.

"Excuse me," she says. "We're talking." She turns her back on me. I massage her rigid shoulders for the two seconds it takes her to slide off the stage away from me. "Just because you're an anomaly of nature doesn't mean we all are," she says.

"You can't catch it from casual contact," I say.

"Catch what?"

"The lesbo-virus."

Carmen yanks off her platform shoe and hurls it at me. Sadly for her, she throws like a girl. I catch the red-beaded thing with one hand and pinch my nose. "A very ancient and fish-like smell," I say before tossing it on top of a high speaker out of reach. Eva looks up from her script and scowls at me.

Nico makes no move to rescue her shoe. I like that in a boy. "My shoulders are a little stiff today," he mumbles.

I press my thumbs in the space between his scapula and spine. His muscles feel like river rocks through his shirt. When Andie arrives, she winks at me and starts to massage my back. She's strong, despite her small hands and slender wrists. Jonathan comes in and joins the chain. No wonder people think Californians are nuts. Then Carmen ruins it by massaging Jonathan. Must she pursue every single person of the male persuasion in the tri-county area?

Fortunately, Sapphire calls us to start before I think up an evil plan to put her in her place. Bryan goes on first and bounds around the stage, posting love notes to me on chairs representing trees in the forest. After he dashes away, Jonathan—as Touchstone—exchanges witticisms with a shepherd. I walk on next and read one of Bryan's love poems:

From the east to western Ind,
No jewel is like Rosalind.
Her worth—

"Did someone take my script?" Eva interrupts loudly.

"Quiet, please," Sapphire says.

I launch into my poem again, but halfway through, Eva's watch alarm goes off.

"Sorry," she says, feigning confusion. When I begin for the third time, I'm so out of the zone that I sound as flat as a rice paddy.

When Eva enters the scene to tell me that the love of my life has appeared in the forest, I say, "Dost thou think, though I am caparisoned like a man, I have a doublet and hose in my disposition? I prithee tell me who is it quickly—" at which point her cell bursts into song.

"I forgot to turn it off," she says. Sapphire confiscates it anyway.

In the next part, Bryan and I are alone onstage. Rosalind, disguised as a man, offers to cure Orlando of his hopeless love for Rosalind. I should enjoy this scene, but with all the interruptions, I'm performing on par with a zombie in a B-movie. I can read regret all over Sapphire's face written in Day-Glo marker. She wishes she gave the lead to Eva.

Sapphire ambushes me after rehearsal. "Can we talk?"

"I'm memorizing my lines," I say. It comes out harsh, like I'm talking through ice that I've ground into slush with my teeth. Ever since that day in the bathroom when she hemmed and hawed over Jonathan's sexual orientation, I've demoted her to the realm of unfathomable and irritating adults.

"Can we talk about your new persona? It's not like you to keep things from me."

"You don't tell me everything. You never mentioned a sister."

"We're estranged."

"What does that mean?"

"We've barely spoken in years. You can ask about it another time. This conversation is about you. I thought you were head over heels for the opposite sex."

I meet her gaze at last, taking in her friendly eyes filled with questions. My teeth warm up a little. "I am crazy about boys. I'm just expanding my options. It's not carved in stone, or anything." *And if you say I'm confused, I'll deck you.*

Thankfully, she gets it. "Okay, then. And about the play . . . you're capable of being an amazing Rosalind. Don't let the others destroy your focus."

"No problem," I say. "Tomorrow I'll send your socks into orbit."

The next morning I take the DykeByke from its hiding place under my bed and throw it out the window. I will ride it to school today to prove to Eva I'm not a coward. Still, there's no point in acting the clotpole by wheeling it through the house. Dad didn't take it well when I mentioned the *L* word during our haircut chat. Besides, hate vandalism makes lousy breakfast conversation. I wash down my microwave Tofurky sausage with soy milk, worrying a bit about the effect of soybeans on mental health.

When I zip into the school parking lot—early for once—an unwelcome scene awaits me. Jonathan and Carmen are holding hands under the big olive tree.

Something is rotten in the state of California. Translation? Reality keeps wrecking my life. I could survive sharing him with a cute boy, or just about anybody else in the world. As I watch them disappear together through the cafeteria door—his hand now on her waist—my thoughts turn to war.

I hang by the door to the cafeteria waiting for them to come out. When they emerge at last, they're still in holding-hands mode. I follow them at a discreet distance. They finally part ways, and there is no swapping of spit at least. But in homeroom, my morning plunges further south. A limerick covers the entire dry-erase board. The letters are so large that a nearsighted person from the planet Myopia could read it. The war started without me.

There onZ was a dyke-grrl named RoZ
Who would do anything for apploZ
She tried to kiss all her friendZ
And pat their rear endZ
Beware! Dont get caught in her cloZ

Carmen has a dangerous stillness to her. Think the eye of a hurricane. I have no doubt she is responsible. My only hope is that Jonathan wasn't present when she wrote it because that would be the unkindest cut of all. Andie fails me by not showing up, and Nico turns the knife by copying down the low-class verse into his notebook. He doesn't look up when I call him a name. Even Mr. Beltz has the audacity to smile before erasing it.

My feverish effort to compose an equally offensive verse in honor of Carmen consumes the remainder of the homeroom eon. I allow myself one grim snort that could be called a laugh when I rhyme *cafeteria* with *bacteria.* My poem, the embodiment of the Platonic Ideal of Nastiness, is complete when the bell rings. I hurry to the Barn to copy it onto scroll paper. When I finish, I tuck it in with the other scrolls to be used later.

I haven't spoken to a soul this morning, unless you count the uncivil words to Nico in homeroom. So I call Andie's cell between my next two classes, adopting a radio voice when she answers. "If your name is Andie Orlov, you've just won a two-year supply of Thor condoms. They come in Bodacious Blue and Orgasm Orange." For all her wild eyeliner, clothing, and opinions on sexuality, she's very shy when the subject of actual sex comes up.

"A two-year supply?"

"They come in boxes of one thousand."

"That means I'll need, let me see, zero," she says.

"Hi," I say. "Where were you? Are you?"

"I'll make it to school by rehearsal. What's up?"

"Did you know that Jonathan and Carmen are love-birds?"

"Liar," she says.

"I know something you don't know," I chant like a second-grade taunt.

"Do not," she says. I like the way she argues.

"Do so."

"Prove it."

"If I prove that Carmen and Jonathan are sucking face in secret, you have to tell me everything you know about everyone. Deal?"

"Deal. Except what do I get if you're wrong?"

"I know what I saw," I say, but she interrupts before I give her the details.

"Sure you see things, but you don't really SEE. That's why you have no idea what's going on."

BlueDragon waddles over to where I'm spazzing out. "There's someone NICE who LIKES me who wants to talk to me. Bye." I hang up and scratch BlueDragon's ears. Maybe I should compose a limerick to Andie next.

By rehearsal time, I'm lonely, and in the spirit of loneliness, I make a tiny confession to myself. Andie is right; I don't understand anyone or anything. Now that Jonathan is dead to me, my only friends (is that even the right word?) are Machiavelli meets Mata Hari and Cousin Itt.

Eva—Why has she shut me out?

Jonathan—How could he get smoochy with the anti-Roz?

Carmen (the anti-Roz)—Why does everyone choose her over me?

Andie (Machiavelli meets Mata Hari)—Where do I even begin?

Bryan—If he's into me, why doesn't he break up with Eva?

Okay, the last question is a tad superficial, but enquiring minds need to know. The tabloid headline could read: WORLD'S OLDEST MAN ASKS WORLD'S OLDEST WOMAN ON FIRST DATE. I HAVE WAITED A HUNDRED YEARS FOR

THIS MOMENT, SHE SAYS. I slink into the shadows at the back of the stage, pretending to be engrossed in my script while keeping an eye on the happenings around me.

Nico sits slumped over on the edge of the stage. The swath of hair curtaining his face stirs a little as Andie whispers into his ear. When Eva puts her arm around Bryan's waist, Carmen sits abruptly in Nico's lap. Nico sinks down a little under her weight, but doesn't move a muscle. Think compost. Okay, maybe one person in the world would choose me over Carmen.

"New jacket?" Andie asks Carmen.

"Yes," Carmen says. "Don't you adore faux fur? It's so PC." She strokes the collar like it's mink.

The word *sweatshop* comes to mind. I clamp my lips together to keep from shouting it. Nico pushes Carmen off his lap and stands up.

"A child made your coat for twenty cents an hour," he says.

I dig the synchronicity. Maybe I'm being harsh calling him Cousin Itt.

"And you are as pure as the driven snow." Without warning, Carmen turns back his shirt collar to read the tag.

Nico's eyes are hidden on account of his hair, but his lips look smug. "I buy American."

Carmen grabs at the waistband of his underwear with lightning speed. "Made in Pakistan," she crows.

Nico pulls away from her. "Hey, my grandma buys my underwear," he says.

Bryan hoots. "Your grandma?"

I struggle to keep my eyes on the script. My Gandhi-and-Me side thinks Nico is sexy-cool for being political about his clothes. My social radar side says he's a dweeb for announcing that his grandma buys his underwear, and a double-dweeb for *letting* his grandma buy his underwear. He's back to Cousin Itt.

Warm hands cover my eyes from behind. I smell Sapphire's patchouli soap.

"Whatcha doing in the dark, Pixie?" Jonathan says.

My heart swells. Despite the fling with Carmen, he's still my friend.

"Pixie," I say, "that's cute. I like that in a nickname. Use that one from now on."

"Will do, Shrimp."

I laugh. "Andie says that if I want to understand people, I have to shut up and observe them. So I'm watching today instead of hanging out. All has been revealed. Everyone's crazy. Especially you."

"I can see you are in a mood," he says. "I'll be moving along now."

I grab his wrist. "Not before you tell me Sapphire's real name."

"Sedona," he says, and then grins at me.

"I see that you're going to be tight-lipped about this. I bet you won't tell me what you were doing with Ms. Low-cut Sweater before school either."

Jonathan's grin vanishes. "What's your problem?" he growls.

I have no small talent for making conversation go south. Why can't I keep that sharp tongue of mine in its sheath? Note to self: Destroy the scroll with my love poem to Carmen before Jonathan sees it. I want to hear him call me Pixie again.

"She isn't always the nicest to me," I mumble.

Sapphire arrives and calls us to take our places. I pour all my misery and confusion into Rosalind's lines. When my scenes flow well for once, a smudge of confidence grows inside me. With each well-acted line, a petal of my blossom unfolds. At the break, I step outside the Barn so I won't be distracted by the little conversations. I want to stay in the zone. The thick fog makes me feel as if I walked into the witches' scene in *Macbeth*.

But my new confidence doesn't last because when I go back into the Barn, the furled scrolls are hanging from the rafters. Panic knocks the blossom right out of me.

"I thought we'd try the scrolls early," Sapphire says. "Give the stage techs a chance to work out the kinks so they might actually work on opening night."

I should leave now. But that will only make me look guilty. If I'm lucky, the ropes will tangle. But they don't. My poem unfurls perfectly near the end of the scene. Maybe no one will actually read it. But everyone does. I kiss my shiny new nickname courtesy of my former friend Jonathan good-bye.

Darling Carmen,
There once was a she-dog in heat
Who chased every boy she did meet
She lured them to the cafeteria
(Despite the bacteria)
And ate them, except for their feet

A few geeks laugh until Sapphire, her ears back and tail twitching, stares them down.

"Fess up," she says.

Carmen drops to her knees on the stage in front of Sapphire. "I'm so very sorry," she says through her tears. "I started the whole thing. I posted a vicious limerick about Roz in homeroom because I'm so jealous of her. Please don't force me out of the play."

"I'm afraid I have no choice," Sapphire says.

Like that could happen. My invented scene stretches even the limits of Roz Fantasy Land.

"Fess up," Sapphire says, looking right at me.

"I don't believe in limericks," I say. A giant laughter-sucking vacuum empties the Barn of all sound.

"This has to stop," Sapphire says.

"Why is everyone looking at moi?" I say. "I didn't do it."

"The play is canceled."

The silence deepens. It reminds me of the moment in an old movie I saw once when the doctor pulled out the bone saw to amputate a limb without anesthesia.

"Please," I say.

"The mean pranks are only one part of why I'm canceling the play. I have to go away next week. On family business. If I leave you to your own devices, I'll come back to find your skeletons scattered across the stage."

Eva steps forward and clears her throat. "Almost everyone has had it in for Roz since she got the lead. Me included."

"Go on," Sapphire says.

"Her prank was a reaction to someone else's prank, which was a reaction . . . well, you get the idea."

Although she doesn't say Carmen's name, only a clotpole could miss the implication.

"I'm sorry that it got out of hand. If someone can direct

while you're gone, I promise we'll work together like a team. You can check in by phone every day."

"Well," Sapphire says. We hold our breath while she considers. "Okay, Eva will direct. If I catch the faintest whiff of unkind behavior at rehearsals, it's curtains for the production. I have my spies. We're done for today."

I'm torn between throwing myself at Eva's feet in gratitude and tearing out her eyes from envy. Director, no less. The Diva triumphs again. Before I can do either, our savior clamps my wrist and drags me toward the door.

"Andie," I yell over my shoulder, "if you haven't heard from me by tomorrow, call in the National Guard." Eva stops at a copse behind the Barn. It's a few degrees above freezing, and I don't have a jacket.

"I can't believe you did that," Eva says.

"Since when did Carmen become a candidate for sainthood? Like you said, she started it." I am already drizzle-moistened and shivering. "Besides, I thought you weren't even talking to her."

Eva sighs. "She was my best friend before that. Ease up on her a little."

"Shall I keep your hogs and eat husks with them?" I say. I stomp my feet to stave off the cold. "Tell her to ease up on *me*."

"There's a reason. . . ." She inhales like she might actually tell me something. A big thing. An important thing. About Carmen. I try to look as trustworthy as Yoda.

"What?" I ask. The fog seeps through my thin sweater. Eva rubs my hands between hers. While she has me trapped, she exhales slowly in my face like the divas of old, except it's water vapor instead of cigarette smoke.

"If I tell you something," she says, "you have to swear on your life—no, that's too puny—you have to swear on your ambition to be the next Julia Roberts that you'll never tell a soul."

This is it. The wall is coming down. But will the truth hurt? "I swear," I whisper.

"On your ambition."

"May Hollywood forever shun me."

"And Broadway, too."

"And Broadway, too," I repeat.

"A while back, before our fight, Carmen told me that she's a lesbian," she says.

This takes many long seconds to penetrate my circuitry because it never occurred to me before. Then, as I try to integrate this new fact into all that I know, my brain bogs down like a computer with too many programs running in the background. "Oh," I say at last.

Eva nods.

"Oh," I say again. "That's why she detests Bryan. She's in love with you and can't stand that you're with him."

"Maybe," she says.

Eva has a hat and scarf in addition to her warm coat. I capture the hat easily, but the tassels on the scarf get tangled in her hair. She takes it off and winds it around my neck.

"And the whole flirty act," I say. "She dresses like a slut so no one will guess."

"You do have a handful of gray matter after all. I was wrong about you, Chub."

"I've lost five pounds," I say.

She doesn't understand what I mean. Calling me Chub must be a reflex for her.

"You'll leave her alone now that you know," she says. She grabs hold of the scarf and chokes me lightly. "Don't blab it around. She's afraid her mom will disown her. I don't trust you. Here's your chance to prove me wrong."

The calculator in my head keeps adding things up. "Did she say she was bi?"

"She's not bi," Eva says.

"But she could like boys."

"Girl plus girl equals lesbian, Chub."

"What about Jonathan?"

"What about him?"

"If Carmen's a lesbian, why is she Jonathan's new girlfriend?"

"What?" Eva makes a face like the star in a daytime soap when her ex-husband's evil twin comes back from the dead. Then a slow smile spreads across her face. "I get it. You're joking." She takes back her hat. "Good one, scrambled-eggs-for-brains."

"*What happened at school* today?" Mom asks over dinner.

Let's see now. Jonathan went to the cafeteria to make out with Carmen. Carmen ambushed me with a limerick in homeroom. I retaliated. Sapphire almost canceled the play. Eva informed me that Carmen is an undercover lesbian.

"I have to write an essay on a historical figure," I say. "I'm thinking Amelia Earhart." These irrelevant tidbits make Mom believe she knows what's going on in my life. I bolt the rest of my dinner to escape more questions and Dad's brooding stares. Eva follows suit.

"Dishes, girls," Mom says.

"I promised to help Roz with math tonight," Eva says.

Only she didn't. Fortunately, I catch on fast. "Yeah, trig's a beast," I say. Mom will clean up herself rather than interfere with a sibling bonding opportunity.

My sister winks at me. The Three Faces of Eva. I'm a slave to hope, so I risk being alone with her. One locked door later, she fixes me with her interrogator's smile.

"Forgot your promise yet?"

"It's only been a few hours," I say. "But I'll take the secret to my grave. Why don't you trust me?"

She grins at me. From her rakish look I can tell that I'm in for it. "You know how some people have an angel on one shoulder and a devil on the other? Well . . . your angel hangs out around your heart. But your devil is in charge of your tongue." Her phone twitters just then, and she checks the call.

I'm glad for the diversion because my throat suddenly hurts like I swallowed a fish bone. What she said is true, of course, and the list goes on—self-absorbed, competitive, and insecure. Still, I wish I could be perfect in her eyes. At least she sees the angel in my heart.

"Let's get started on that trig homework," I say when she closes her phone.

She laughs at that. My fish-bone moment escaped her notice. She drops a plain manila envelope in my lap. I open the clip and two magazines with racy covers slide out onto the bed. One shows a woman wearing chaps and not much else leaning against a horse. The other features a man with chiseled abs wearing micro undies and a baseball cap. He's staring at me like I'm Aphrodite in the flesh.

"What's this?" I ask.

"Porn," Eva says.

"Duh. Why are you giving it to me?"

"I thought it might help you figure out where you are on the dashboard." She arranges them side by side on her desk, watching me closely for a reaction. "They won't jump up and rip off your clothes," she says.

My eyes have trouble focusing.

"Well?"

"The lighting in here isn't quite right," I say.

"Keep them. But if Mom discovers them in your room, I know nothing." Her computer clicks away, nibbling on electronic potato chips. "I don't want her to think I'm tacky."

"You don't have to explain," I say. "Is it weird that your ex–best friend has a crush on you?"

"Not that weird."

"How did she tell you exactly? Did she come on to you?"

"I have things to do," Eva says, dismissing me with her diva wave.

Talking to her is like eating Jell-O with a fork. Just when you're about to pop the yummy bite into your mouth, it slips off the tines and splats on the floor.

The magazines glow red-hot on my desk, despite my effort to ignore them. I turn on my computer to distract me. I think about what Eva said—that I have a devil in charge of my tongue. My persistent case of big-fat-mouthitis probably does affect my friendships a little. Then again, Sierra used to laugh her head clean off her shoulders around me. I check my email, but she hasn't written back yet.

Am I a good friend? There's an online quiz to test your friendship quotient, so I take it and pass without cheating. To be honest, I won't stay friends forever with someone who constantly needs me, and I don't share every detail of my life, especially my mistakes. Who needs to be liked by the whole world and their cousin? I don't like every single person on the planet, either. But a little more kindness to balance out my less tactful side couldn't hurt. I vow to work on it.

The second I figure out who I am.

With the door locked and the lights off, I make a tent out of my covers and climb inside with a flashlight and Eva's porn. I skip the articles and go straight for the pictures. Neither photo spread tickles me all that much. Maybe the unnatural poses remind me that the models were under hot lights and in front of cameramen. Ugh. The guys are hunky and the girls are curvy, but in the end they're only strangers. I consider burning the magazines in the field next to our house. With my luck, though, a volunteer fire fighter would happen to be lost in our neighborhood at just the wrong moment.

The residual pot smoke clinging to Eyeliner Andie in homeroom escapes everyone's notice somehow. The beads she sewed onto the tattered fringe of her jeans jacket click as she shifts in her seat.

"I have a plan," she whispers. "To stop Carmen from hanging all over Nico."

"I think we should be nice to Carmen from now on," I say.

"What's with you?" she says.

"I feel sorry for her."

"Okay, we'll be friendlier," she says. "After I'm through with her."

"What are you going to do?"

"You're not usually such a kiss-ass."

Mr. Beltz shakes his pointer at us, and we revert to hand signals to continue our conversation. I pucker my lips to prove that I mean to suck up. Andie makes the universal loco sign. I flip her off. She bares her teeth at me. I see Mr. Beltz approaching and slice a finger across my throat. She doesn't see me in time, screws up her eyes, and sticks out her tongue. For some unfathomable reason, her tongue is bright blue.

"Maybe you girls would like to move your performance to the front of the class," he says.

"No, thank you," I say in a polite-little-girl voice.

Carmen snickers at us. When Andie raises her hand to give Carmen the bird, I grab it. Andie's friendship style could be called more cactus than fuzzy bear. Still, I don't have to dodge spines around her because I'm almost positive she's on my side. More or less.

After Mr. Beltz has retreated to the front of the class, Andie writes a few words in her notebook for me to see. *I'm doing her a favor today. You'll see.*

As I approach the cafeteria dishwasher, competing smells—eau d'aging dishcloth and a miasma of chemical disinfectant—assault my nose. Felicia shows me how to fill the racks with dirty trays and then leaves me alone to suffer. Twenty minutes of mouth breathing later, she returns and tells me to empty the deep fryer.

"Please don't spill the oil all over the floor," she says. It's the "please" that gets me, and I do my best. After I clean up the oil slick, she calls me to the break table and slides a plate in front of me. At the center rests a leather brown disk.

"What's this?" I say.

"A meatless patty," she says. "The first thing on my new vegetarian menu. Enjoy." She sits down next to me with a mug of coffee.

The thing cuts like leather too. "Muy delicioso," I say.

Her smile beams intermittently like a flickering motel sign.

"You're not a whiner," she says. "I hate whiners."

I chew the first bite for a long time before swallowing. Felicia might not be up on the Heimlich maneuver. "Thanks," I say.

"Or a quitter. I have a daughter your age. She could learn something from you." She slurps her coffee.

I won her over, and that means a lot to me. Maybe I'm not a big hit with the pep squad, the football team, or even the German club. I'm not always the most popular with my homies the theater geeks either. But I managed to bridge some serious gap with a cafeteria worker. Make that Cafeteria Commando. When she leaves, I wrap up the remains of the pucklike patty in a napkin for Blue-Dragon.

At rehearsal we roll through two whole scenes without a single crumb of harassment. Whenever Andie and Nico are offstage, though, they go into a corner together and giggle like preteens at a slumber party. This worries me because I know they are plotting against Carmen. Instead of crashing their party or braving the chill from the ice man formerly known as Jonathan, I pretend to want to hang out by myself.

After the last scene, Sapphire leaves us to clean up. Eva and Carmen have a brief public conversation for the first time since their fight. A minute later, Nico abruptly stops sweeping the stage and points at something brown near his foot.

"Who let BlueDragon in here?" When several geeks move in for a closer look, he picks up the turd with his bare hands.

"Eww. That's so gay," Carmen says.

"What exactly do you mean by that?" I say.

"Don't be obtuse. Everyone knows that *gay* doesn't mean *gay*. It means *gross*."

You must really hate yourself. My thoughtless tongue almost gets away from me, but I manage to stop it in time.

Next Nico sniffs the brown thing in his hand, and a chorus of horrified noises lifts the roof off the Barn. The rest happens as if in slow motion. He raises it to his lips and bites into one end. Several geeks scream. Andie's usually pale face glows scarlet. She's about to pop from hilarity. When Nico takes a second bite and says, "Yum," there's a mass stampede out the door. I'm left alone with Andie, Nico, and the dog doo.

"Carmen will NEVER touch you again," Andie gasps out between bouts of hysteria.

My face must be a frozen mask of disgust because Nico holds out the remaining half of the pooplike object for my inspection. "It's a hazelnut energy bar. Andie shaped it."

Oh, great. The one boy in a hundred-mile radius crushing on me couldn't be normal?

"Good one," I say. "Later."

Eva calls Mom to say that she'll be eating dinner at Carrie the Cheery Cheerleader's house. I happen to know that Carrie flew to Minnesota for a cousin's wedding, but I keep my mouth shut for the second time today. It feels good. Knowledge is power.

"I'm glad she's branching out after this whole Carmen thing," Mom says.

The meal passes like a trig class in slow motion, while my mind whirrs and clicks in hyperkinetic mode. If Eva isn't with Carrie, where is she? Maybe with Carmen. Carmen could be propositioning her while I eat onion soup. Carmen could be trying to kiss her while I chew on my last crouton. After clearing the table, I hear Eva's Honda hacking in the driveway. I sprint from the kitchen to the driver's-side door before she can get away.

The skin around her eyes looks puffy. "Go away," she says when she sees me.

"What's wrong? Prithee, speak, my poor child," I say.

"I said GO AWAY."

She opens her bedroom window and climbs through, slamming down the sash behind her. There's a problem with the "knowledge is power" thing. I don't know anything.

Back in my room I flip on my computer because it's always willing to talk to me. Right now I need a heartwarming coming-out story to soothe my ragged nerves. With Jonathan in mind, I enter "African-American gay teen." After a long and almost fruitless search, I discover that a lot of black lesbians pour their hearts out online. Black gay boys do not. I score only one story, posted by Derek.

> The church has always been a big part of my life. The fear of losing it, and of losing my family and friends, kept me quiet for a long time. I was afraid to disappoint anyone. But when I finally came out to them, our connection grew stronger. I had forgotten how important honesty is

to good living. Some of the people I care about joined my new church, and that showed me the depth of their feelings.

My cell rings and I reach for it. It's Bryan.

Me: Hey. *(Still a little choked up from the story.)*
Him: Hey. Been thinking about you.

Wherefore the sexy rock-star voice? Omigod.

Me: What exactly about me?

Does he notice the squeak at the end of my question?

Him: Ready for the real thing? Let's go for a drive after rehearsal.

M-o-n-u-m-e-n-t-a-l. Bryan asking me on a date + Eva crying in her room = they broke up.

Me: What do you mean?
Him: Just you and me.

While I consider this, my heart booms louder than a tuba in a marching band. Eva and I had many firsts together—first rotten peach fight, first time skinny-dipping at the reservoir, first time roller-blading under a cow at a fair. Then rumor had it she went all the way with Bryan when I didn't even have a boyfriend.

Me: We should take it slow.
Him: Whatever you want.
Me: I don't want to hurt Eva.
Him: Me either.

Chapter 17

After Bryan's bombshell, my online Ouija session goes like this:

Should I take a drive with Bryan? YES

Is Bryan serious about me? YES

Would Eva be upset if she found out? YES

Should I go anyway? YES

It's unanimous. Living a guilt-free life involves too much self-sacrifice for my taste. Unfortunately, guilt causes my nervous mannerisms to attack in force, knee bouncing, cuticle picking, lip chewing—the whole menu. I try breathing into a paper bag. I try tap-dancing. I try tap-dancing while breathing into a bag. Am I dumb enough to risk my new closeness with Eva over some boy? Then again, that boy is Bryan. And if Eva and I really were close, she would've come to cry on my shoulder tonight instead of hiding in her room. And for another thing? She forgave me the other times I went after her ex-boyfriends. Eventually.

I take my cell phone for a walk around the field to clear my head. It likes the fresh air. It likes talking to Andie.

Me: For the latest breaking headlines, the RoZ News Channel.
Andie: Hey.
Me: Don't you think Carmen could be bi?
Andie: Stop with the labels, already.
Me: So what makes you think she isn't Jonathan's girlfriend?
Andie: I know what I know.
Me: I prithee take the cork out of thy mouth, that I may drink thy tidings.
Andie: If you come over after rehearsal tomorrow, I might give you a few hints.
Me: Sorry. Too much homework.

Homework in the backseat of Bryan's car.

As I near Sapphire's house, a dot of orange glowing through the blackness suggests that Jonathan is smoking outside.

Me: Got to go. Later.

I drift over and drop down on the porch step next to him ever so casually. "Don't you know that smoking gives you STDs?" I grab his cigarette and stomp it out.

"Thanks for saving me," he says. The angle of his neck reads dejected.

Whenever we're together like this, breathing the same air in and out, I almost come clean about Eva's dare. He's the only one I feel guilty about deceiving. But my good sense of timing prevents me from being honest. Before yesterday we were having too much fun together. And now he's too moody. Confessing would be a selfish act, and he might not understand.

I toss and catch the pack of cigarettes before offering it to him. "Go ahead. Give yourself gonorrhea," I say.

He ignores my attempt to lighten the mood. "Lay off Carmen, will you?"

"Carmen and I go way back," I say. "Our feud goes way back, I mean." After learning Carmen's secret, I do regret how I've acted toward her. Not that she entirely deserves my sympathy after how she's treated me. And she's using Jonathan as a decoy boyfriend. That isn't exactly nice. "Anyway, our feud is over as of this minute."

He puts a cigarette between his lips and lets it dangle there.

I'm dying to tell him the truth about Carmen, but Eva's assessment of my foot-in-mouth disease keeps getting in the way, not to mention my solemn vow to take the secret to my grave. Jonathan's little romance with her piques my curiosity. There's a limerick about that. A pansy who lives in Khartoum, took a lesbian up to his room. . . . "It's sweet of you to defend your girlfriend," I say.

He brushes his thumb across the lighter.

"So you're going hetero," I say, fishing for how much he knows.

Jonathan claps his free hand over my mouth. He's shaking. "I'm not gay enough for you now?" he says.

He drops his hand again. I can't read his face hidden by shadow. If I try to hug him, he might reject me. Or light my hair on fire. "*I* go both ways, too, remember?" His shoulder doesn't yield to my affectionate squeeze.

He jerks away from me. "I'm not black enough. I'm not gay enough."

"I didn't say that. I mean, I'm sorry if I—" But he's already gone, with the door banging behind him, leaving me alone in the dark. Why do I always ruin things when I really care about someone? I start obsessing that my feelings are flowing down a one-way street, and I panic.

I creep back across the field through the black night. With my luck, P. Tom will accost me before I make it home. "And I thought I was a mess," he'll say.

My American history class lets out early. I cruise to the Barn before rehearsal starts, hoping to surprise someone in the act. Anyone. Any act. I'm not picky. The place is deserted, but someone came ahead of me because a crudely made sign sits by the door: QUIT THE PLAY ROZ OR YOU'LL COME TO A BAD END. Yellow-green paint drips like alien drool down the scrap of plywood, an authentic touch that gives me the heebies. Still, I have to hide it quick before Sapphire sees. Carmen must be beyond desperate to pull a stunt like this.

By the time the theater geeks start arriving, I've stashed the sign behind some props in the area we affectionately call backstage. Andie comes in, and I drag her off to a private corner to talk to her. The metallic red eyeliner and dark purple lip goop she has on says vampire. When she opens her mouth, I expect fangs.

"Who did the sign?" I whisper.

She looks at me curiously. "What sign?"

"Never mind." Hah! I detect a crack in her perfect knowledge.

She shakes her head. "I've got something to show you." She removes a bit of paper from under the band on her funky blue hat. It's a photograph of Nico in profile on a rock next to a river, his hair sleeked back like he just came out of the water. No shirt. He looks hot, and I'm not talking about the weather.

"Madam, I come to whet your gentle thoughts on his behalf," she says.

"Hmmm," I say, slipping the photo in my bag. Oh, great. Now I'm having wanton thoughts about the weird boy. What next? Andie looks hot too. If you have a thing for ghouls.

"There's Jonathan," I say. "I need to talk to him." I bound over like an enthusiastic puppy. Maybe he'll accept my apology this time.

"I don't want to talk to you," he growls.

His hands are splattered with green paint. I back away slowly.

My fantasies are turning toward the Stephen King–esque.

Actually, Jonathan's hands are clean. He wouldn't hurt a fly. A beetle maybe, but not a fly. He most definitely wouldn't hurt me.

When I bound over, he says, "I don't want to talk to you. I'm in a mood."

"Just read this," I say, giving him the coming-out story I found on the Net.

Sapphire makes an entrance. Everyone quiets down.

"I leave tonight," she announces. "I'll be gone all next week. Jonathan, too."

Oh. So maybe his mood isn't just about me.

"Eva was supposed to strut her directorial stuff today," Sapphire continues. "Unfortunately, she's out sick. What does she have, Roz?"

Eva stayed home from school? "Just a cold," I say, too embarrassed to admit my ignorance.

Sapphire moves a chaise longue to one side on the stage and settles in. "Carmen will direct, and Andie will read Eva's part. Pretend I'm not here and go at it. Act four, scene three."

Carmen looks like she just died and was reincarnated as Sofia Coppola. That's when I notice a faint sprinkling of green paint on her sexy mesh sleeve. Before, I suspected. Now, I have proof. I contemplate which violent death would be best for her, but after the bear pit, the poisoning, and the beheading, my thoughts take a new direction. Carmen risked Sapphire's wrath and the demise of the play for the slim chance of playing the lead. How sad is that?

The poor girl has become completely unhinged. Maybe Carmen lied to her mom and told her she got the lead. In that case, she'd have to do anything she could to make that happen. Including bumping me off. My insides become a tangle of annoyance and sympathy coated with a thin layer of fear. Think spaghetti with olive oil.

I try to focus on the play. In the first part of the next scene, Nico delivers a letter from Carmen wherein she declares her love for me, a woman disguised as a man.

"She has a leathern hand," I say about Carmen after reading the letter. "I verily did think that her old gloves were on, but 'twas her hands." Feeling sorry for Carmen doesn't have to dampen the pleasure of insulting her in the play.

Bryan looks at me like he can't wait to devour me after rehearsal. I forget about Carmen then and start obsessing about my secret date with him. My internal spaghetti gets so knotted up, I'm forced to try a relaxation technique Sierra taught me. You're supposed to picture yourself in a soothing place far away. But when I close my eyes, the picture that comes—Bryan kissing me in his car—only makes my pulse rev faster.

Despite my yummy daydream, I'm dimly aware of the rehearsal going on around me. Oliver (played by Noah, a theater geek I haven't mentioned because he's not terribly interesting) comes out of the forest clutching a handkerchief soaked in Orlando's blood. While he tells the tale of the wounding, he and Andie fall in love at first sight.

"I like the way Andie bent down her head in the scene," Sapphire says. "It gives her the right mix of shy and bold. Tell Eva to try it."

"I'm the director, am I not?" Carmen says.

"Sorry. Carry on."

"Excellent scene." Carmen writes a note on her script. And then reality makes another unwelcome intrusion into my invented life. "Roz! Pay attention. Start downstage for the story and float upstage for the swoon."

In the spirit of niceness, I stow the attitude and comply. Still, Carmen as director falls into a specific category of nightmare—the kind where you're at the front of the school auditorium wearing an undersized coconut bra and plastic hula skirt to debate the relevance of the United Nations. Except you forgot to prepare.

At the end of rehearsal, Sapphire shouts "Bravo! Olé!" She leaves with Jonathan before I can talk to him. Bryan slips out behind them. I know where he's headed. The guilt over my impending tryst taints my euphoria.

Chapter 18

My *invented life is* about to turn real. Sadly, I have to lie about it to my friends and slink out the back to meet it. When I cross the deserted field, the wind blows through the dry grass, whispering *RoZ iZ stalking Eva's ex-boyfriend*.

"We're just going for a drive," I tell the grass, "so shut up." I've made up my mind to limit today's activities to talking. If he tries anything, I'll tell him to keep his hands to himself.

Clouds of exhaust billow from Bryan's ancient Trans Am at the far edge of the back parking lot. Bryan, wherefore art thou Bryan? Translation? I wish I were meeting Romeo instead.

"Get in quick before someone sees," he says. Romeo he's not, in more ways than one.

I duck into the passenger seat.

He shifts into first gear. "I didn't think you'd come." He flashes me the forlorn-puppy look.

Now that he's inches away, his magnetic properties work their magic on me. "Why not?" I say. "You're good to look at and fun to be around."

He laughs and his lips are at their most kissable. Okay, maybe one little make-out session to test my sexual orientation before I put on the brakes.

"What do you see in me?" I ask.

"I don't know," he says.

"You don't know?"

"You make me feel good, I guess."

My hopes and dreams circle the drain. I wasn't exactly expecting, "You're the most beautiful woman on earth, and I love you." Still, he should've at least said, "You're hot, and I'm into you."

He pulls into the old peach orchard at the edge of town. The engine clicks as it cools. He inches toward me. Despite my resolve, I can't resist the touch of his lips. But when I kiss him back, he puts his hands up my shirt. That's when I detect alcohol vapors. Here lies RoZ Peterson, killed in a senseless car wreck with her sister's stupid ex-boyfriend.

I push him away. "You've been drinking."

"I don't believe in alcohol. The bottle is under the seat. Want some?"

I shake my head. This is turning into the date from hell.

Bryan puts his hands into his jacket pockets. "Pick a hand," he says.

"You got me a present?" I ask. "How sweet." As he uncurls his fingers, I gasp. A beautiful ruby ring rests on his palm.

I would have settled for a semiprecious stone. But no.

He opens his hand with a flourish and reveals a foil-wrapped condom.

Both my fists thump the middle of his chest. "I said

slow, Bryan. By my troth, I was seeking for a fool when I found you. You suck romance from a date like a weasel sucks eggs." Translation? Another Roz fantasy bites the dust.

"You knew what I wanted. You want it too."

I roll down my window and drop the condom onto the ground. "My father was no prostitute," I say. "No wonder Eva broke up with you."

The way Bryan bites his lip reveals everything.

"Craven, dissembling rabbit-sucker! You didn't break up with her?" I yell. That makes me the sorry side dish. RoZ iZ coleslaw. I push open the passenger door with my elbow. "I hope you lose all your teeth and hair. I hope you die ugly and alone. Today."

I start marching back toward town. The engine roars to life and he creeps alongside me, *creep* being the operative word.

"I didn't lie," he whines. "I never said I broke up with Eva."

"Mewling coxcomb," I growl without looking his way.

"But I'll break up with her soon."

I'm sick of his excuses and breathing his exhaust. I pick up a rock. He rolls up the window in a hurry. A satisfying cracking noise says I don't throw like a girl. He accelerates abruptly, kicking up a storm of grit.

As I trudge down the lane, I picture myself taking a baseball bat to his precious Trans Am. I slash his tires in my mind. Hell hath no fury like a woman falsely seduced. Translation? I'd rather blame him for my crazy self-deceptions. Soon self-pity takes over from anger. After walking a few miles in my invented shoes, they're giving me blisters. The sad part is how I fooled myself into coming today because I wanted to. But at my core there's a small voice, and if I listen carefully, it speaks the truth. If only I could hook an amplifier to it.

On the outskirts of town, a painful laugh rises from deep inside. I *finally* have proof about Bryan's two-timing, lying ways. Too bad I can't tell Eva without having to explain my role in it. I'll use that as an example of irony in my next English paper. There's a rock in my shoe, and I leave it in for penance. A quarter mile later the Woe-Is-Me channel grows tiresome, and I switch it off. Poor Eva has it worse. Bryan is her *boyfriend*.

After dinner and in the privacy of my room, I write BRYAN #1 ASSHOLE across my arm with a permanent black marker. I write it a second time. Maybe after a thousand repetitions I won't forget. When I've finished covering my left shin, the phone rings. For one mentally ill second, I imagine it's him calling to apologize. I let the phone ring while I work on my other shin.

Saturday morning I hide my body essay on Bryan with a long-sleeved shirt and sweatpants before going to Eva's room. There is no good lie to explain what I wrote. All the perfumes of Arabia will not sweeten this little sister. Translation? If she sees it, I'm screwed.

"L Report," I say at the door.

"Come in," she says. The ab queen is on the floor doing Pilates.

"Why didn't you go to school yesterday?" I ask.

"You should try this exercise," she says. "It's great for the thighs."

If I had her extension I'd do the scissors night and day. I try to follow her next moves. The desire to confess overwhelms me. I squash it the best I can, but a little warning pops out against my will. "You're too good for Bryan." Luckily, the exalted warrior pose forces you to look straight ahead.

"I know," she says.

I lose my balance and fall in a heap on the floor. I expected her to say "Why's that?" or "If he's no good, why do you want him?"

Since I'm on the floor already, I move on to crunches. "Well?" I gasp between reps.

She crunches with me. "Sometimes it's easier to keep things going than to break up." She doesn't stop at fifty (but I do). "And he loves me in his warped way." She has no idea how warped, but she won't hear it from me. Or read clues written on my body. "I'm going to break up with him any day now."

This revelation fills me with awe and bliss. She trusts me with another secret, though I SO don't deserve it. My long sleeves and pant legs are all that separate this glorious moment from disaster. I pull them down tight.

"Why?"

"Not for you, Chub," she says. "And don't give me that indignant-slash-innocent look."

"What look?"

"I'm doing it for me."

I open the window to let in some cool air. Sapphire's lemon yellow VW bug is gone, which means that Jonathan has gone too. In all the crazy aftermath of my beef-witted tryst with Bryan, I forgot to call him. Regret sucks.

"Give me the L Report," Eva says. After two hundred crunches, she's still not winded.

I lie down next to her and follow the next exercise at one quarter speed. "Jonathan's mad at me because of the limerick I wrote for Carmen. I'm totally bummed. I thought we were friends, but he took her side."

"She could use a friend right now."

"I've been nice to her since my promise. Anyway I'm talking about Jonathan, not Carmen. Now he's going home for a week, and I'm not there to support him. I'm worried."

Eva rolls onto her stomach, and I roll too. That's when I spy a stack of printouts under her bed.

"Hey, aren't those *my* coming-out stories—the ones you didn't want?"

She sits up. "I read them because of Carmen."

"And?"

"They're fun."

"I know. Some are so moving, I almost cry when I read them. I wish my coming-out had been real so I could write about it online."

"You are so weird, Roz, there could be a reality TV show about you. *America's Psycho Little Sisters.*"

I think about Jonathan all day Sunday. Getting together with his family could be a good thing. Maybe his parents are accepting him, showing him their love, wrapping him up in it. But I have a bad feeling. Sierra would call it a premonition. I call it worry. He's been acting moody for days, which has to be a sign of anxiety. The statistics on the Web about gay teens are not pretty. Gay teens do worse in school, drop out more, and kill themselves more often than other teens. I log on to my favorite Ouija Web site.

"Is Jonathan safe?" I ask.

I close my eyes and let the mouse drift, opening them when it stops. Instead of choosing yes or no, the spirits picked the letter *F*. I repeat and get the letter *I*. In the end, I have the word *F-I-A-R-Y*. Spirits are notoriously atrocious spellers. Still, this answer has me stumped. Maybe he has a fairy godmother. I stick to this hopeful interpretation because my other ideas—say, self-immolation—don't reassure me. Reading about Joan of Arc in the third grade traumatized me for life. I log out. When the internet fails, there's my cell. I send Jonathan a message.

Me: **sup**

He replies right away.

J: **nt tlking 2 u**
Me: **i know. this is txtng**
J: **lol**
Me: **4give me?**
J: **mayb. gtg**
Me: **ttfn**

So he's alive, but that's all I know. When communication fails, a girl can fall back on frozen desserts. A few bites into my first bowl of ice cream (I planned on thirds, at least), I remember about my diet. I dump it down the garbage disposal and fix myself a tasty feta radicchio salad sprinkled with pine nuts. After I chomp it down like a good little bunny, I ride the DykeByke to the Zip-Stop for a Häagen-Dazs bar.

"Stay and talk," Jenny says. She pats the counter. "Sit."

"What's new?" I say. She throws my wrapper in the trash for me.

"The Peeping Tom has moved on," she tells me. "No Birkenstock footprints for weeks."

"How do you know?"

"My partner's an officer." She smiles.

"That's cool." I lick the chocolate off my fingers.

"It is. Between the gossip from the store and the things my partner tells me, we know almost everything that happens in Yolo Bluffs. I'm kind of sorry the Peeping Tom left, though. I thought we'd become friends. He might know even more than I do."

"I heard he went south," I say, "to the Mecca of breast enhancements."

In homeroom, I lean across Nico to whisper into Andie's ear. "No rehearsal Wednesday. Should we do a private one?" A fine line of purple runs along her silvery green eyeliner.

"My place or yours?" she whispers. The skin on my neck tingles when she flirts with me like that. I pluck at my sleeve.

"I have to drive my grandma to the doctor," Nico says. He catches a glimpse of my essay on Bryan before I can cover it.

Thankfully, Mr. Beltz interrupts us. "Quiet. I have an announcement. Carmen has been accepted into MIT. Congratulations, Carmen."

Nico pushes back my sleeve. "What's this?"

"Nothing." I cover my arm again.

"I don't believe in nothing. Did he do something to you?"

"Nothing."

I look up. Mr. Beltz looms over me, and I can see things that shouldn't be seen. The dried shaving cream that sticks to the underside of his chin is the least of it. "Would you like to make an announcement too?" he asks me.

"Oooh," someone says.

I flash him a plastic, synthetic, apologetic smile. "I was just saying to Nico how happy I am for Carmen."

After class Nico follows me into the hall to pester me some more. I deny all his guesses, though some of them get close to the truth. No point in piling another humiliation onto the ever-growing heap. While I stand my ground, the subject of the essay himself appears. Bryan drags me into an empty room. Nico does not exactly follow us in, but his face accuses me through the tiny pane of glass near the top of the door.

"About Friday," Bryan says. "Things aren't always like they look."

"It looks like you're a jerk to me."

He gets down on one knee (really) and holds my hand like in those pathetic fantasies that used to populate my invented life. "I didn't know what I was doing. You make me so crazy. I can't think straight around you."

He's had me alone for fifteen seconds, and already the heat of his desire softens my steely resolve. I mentally scrub at my skin that reads BRYAN #1 ASSHOLE. The ink darkens the rinse water and swirls down the drain. But Nico hasn't left the window. The fact that he's watching us gives me a pinkie-hold on reality.

"Then break up with her," I say.

"I don't want to hurt her."

One painful punch deserves another. *Knavish coxcomb! She's about to break up with YOU.* I keep that lovely and satisfying secret to myself. My ammo belt clip has just one bullet left.

"I'm not looking for a boyfriend," I say. "Because my girlfriend kisses way better than you do." Unfortunately, the bullet is the size of a gnat.

"Who's your girlfriend?"

"Andie." I look toward the window. Nico grins in a way that says he'll pass this on.

Bryan tries a new approach. He stands close to me and traces my cheek with his finger in a slow and delicious way. I can feel the heat coming off his body. He's the snake charmer, and I'm the snake. He leans in so that his lips hover an inch away from mine. I can't stop myself from closing the gap. A thump on the door breaks my trance. I run and fling it open.

"It's not how it looks," I yell to Nico's retreating back.

Felicia grants me a promotion in the cafeteria kitchen at lunch. Today I'm allowed to open packages of grated cheese for the salad bar. She even smiles when I mention that the scissors are a tad dull. "Use this." She hands me a knife.

"You took your happy pills this morning," Vera of the varicose veins says.

"My daughter got accepted at MIT."

The knife slips out of my hand and comes within inches of impaling my foot.

"You must be so proud of her," Vera says.

"No. She's lazy. I don't know why they accepted her. And I'll have to take an evening job to pay her tuition unless several scholarships come through."

I retrieve the knife from the floor. "What's your daughter's name?" I ask.

Felicia closes down. Think heavy velvet curtains dropping unexpectedly before the scene comes to an end.

Vera gives me a dirty look. "Careful with that knife," she says. So cafeteria ladies can do double entendre. Who knew?

"She goes to another school," Felicia says.

Though I've been blind, I'm no fool. Carmen got into MIT, and she has Felicia's arched eyebrows.

"*Hey, lover girl,*" Eyeliner Andie says to me before rehearsal starts. "Nico told me all about our affair. I'm glad I kiss better than Bryan."

"Prove it," I say, and pull her into my arms.

She ducks out of my embrace. "I hate public displays."

"Behind the props, then."

"Get away from me, you lech," says the girl who sews bits of fishnet stocking over the holes in her jeans. "If you must have something in your mouth, chew on this." She gives me a deep blue gumball.

An awkward silence follows. When I picture myself blurting out Felicia's secret, the juicy story turns to dust in my mouth. I hate how empathy interferes with malicious gossip. Poor Carmen. Having your mother work in the cafeteria at your school tops the list of Ten Things More Embarrassing Than Discovering a Piece of Dried Snot on Your Cheek After Talking to Your Crush. And Felicia isn't any ordinary cafeteria worker; she's more like a wolf in midget's clothing. As if the whole undercover lesbian-slash-unrequited-love thing wasn't sad enough.

Eva interrupts my reverie to command us. We need to

run through act 3, scene 2 for the third time. Bryan watches me from the right-hand wing. His soul is in torment because I rejected him. Maybe I should put him out of his misery, but before I get a chance, the scene starts blah, blah, blah. I swallow my gum and enter reading one of Orlando's love poems. The court fool mocks me.

"Sweetest nut hath sourest rind, such a nut is Rosalind," the substitute Touchstone says.

"When there's dyke love on your mind, go hook up with Rosalind," Bryan says.

Eva laughs so hard she falls off her director's chair. "Good one," she says when she catches her breath. "Let's change the script."

Blame the blue food coloring in the gum for my hallucination.

Actually the opposite happens. After Bryan recites his rude verse, Eva takes my side.

"Cut! You're history, Bryan," she says. "Nico plays Orlando today."

You could hear lip gloss being applied in the silence. Bryan gives Eva his patented squishy-snuggle-bunny look. "I was kidding," he says. "Roz can take it. She's tough."

Nico takes a break from combing his hair over his eyes. "No, she's not," he says.

"I told you to leave," Eva says.

Sulky Boy drops his script on the stage and descends the steps two at a time like he's late for an aftershave commercial.

"Your line, Touchstone," Eva says.

"This is the very false gallop of verses," Touchstone says. "Why do you infect yourself with them?"

"Peace, you dull fool! I found them on a tree," I say.

When he comes back at me with, "Truly the tree yields bad fruit," it takes all my self-control to keep from cracking up, even though the substitute Touchstone doesn't hold a candle to Jonathan. Eva's bold move in my defense inflates me till I'm a balloon high above it all shouting, SHE LOVES ME.

At the end of the scene, Eva looks drained. She rests with her head in her hands.

"How shall we proceed?" Carmen asks.

"A short break," Eva says.

Nico, Andie, and I retreat to the zone behind the speakers. We lie on our backs with our heads together.

"I love hiding here," Andie says. "I can't stand it when people look at me."

"So what's your plan on opening night?" I say.

"That's different. I'm not Andie onstage. I'm Audrey. Besides, I act for me. The audience can screw themselves for all I care."

"How would you explain your clothes, then?" I say.

"The clothes are for me too."

While I ponder this perspective so different from my own, Eva descends upon us. "You two took a drive to the peach orchard, didn't you?" Eva says. Everyone knows what the peach orchard means.

"Did not!" Nico and Andie say in unison, misunderstanding the charges.

"None of your business," I add.

"I think it is," she says.

"Excuse us a minute." I jump up and push Eva out the side door.

We face off under the trees. "Bryan told me you dragged him there," Eva says.

I cross my big toe with the index toe of my left foot in preparation for lying. "That *plume-plucked lout*. And you believed him?" I could mention that she's about to break up with him anyway, but that would make me look guilty. I try a silent but honest plea instead. *Okay, we took a short drive and kissed a little before the condom incident, but that's all. And I swear on my future Oscar that I'll never do it again, if only I can get away with it this one last time.*

Eva cups my chin with her fingers. She looks at me long and hard.

"Thanks for taking my side against Bryan today," I say.

"You're welcome." She spins me around and bumps my backside with her knee. "Go hang with your boyfriend and your girlfriend."

Andie looks at me expectantly when I get back. "Who did you go to the peach orchard with? Bryan?"

"The dog," I say. "I took the dog for a walk in the peach orchard."

Andie hoots with laughter. "You don't even have a dog," she shrieks.

"I didn't say it was MY dog."

Nico retreats behind his hair.

When Eva calls us to start again, she still looks pale. She massages her forehead. "I have a headache," she says.

"You should go home," I say. "Carmen can fill in for you." Everyone stares at me in disbelief, like I just morphed into a five-foot-ten-inch hot dog. Especially Carmen. "I'm serious," I say. "Carmen did great last Friday."

"Okay," Eva says. She picks up her bag and leaves.

Carmen immediately goes on a rampage against me. I can hardly blame her for mistrusting my motives. "Is that gum concealed in your mouth?" she asks.

It is. Andie gave me a second gumball during the break.

"No." I swallow hard. "I don't believe in gum." I open my mouth wide and pat my chest like I'm choking on a huge wad. Everyone laughs, even Carmen. After that I behave in an exemplary manner. Twenty minutes later, Carmen stops eyeing me like a brown paper bag left on a subway seat by a terrorist. It feels good to swap out my usual cloak and dagger for a halo and scepter.

When Andie and Nico are offstage together, they whisper like lovers or thieves. It reminds me of how they acted before the Great Dog-Doo Incident. I leave them alone. After rehearsal they take off—hand in hand—without saying good-bye. I stay behind to tell Carmen what a good job she's doing as director. She stares at me like I've turned into the giant hot dog again.

"Truce," I say, making my hands into a T.

"I guess," she says. If a psychic had predicted this scene a few days ago, I would've called her a fraud and demanded my money back.

The next day in homeroom Nico stares straight ahead when I say hi to him. Mr. Beltz has his back to us, so I tap Nico's shoulder. He ignores me even when I walk my fingers down his spine.

"What's with him?" I ask Eyeliner Andie.

She shrugs like she doesn't understand. Her bangs are gelled into sideways spikes. She looks like a novelty coat hanger, a cute one. We exchange notes to pass the time. Class ends without Nico budging from Roz-is-less-than-nothing mode. He hovers some yards down the hall, waiting for Andie to stop talking to me.

"Is this part of some new scheme of yours?" I ask her.

"Brilliant observation," she says.

"But you won't tell me what it is."

"You are so right," she says. "Don't bother your pretty little head with it."

"As long as it doesn't involve eating any unidentifiable objects."

The second bell rings. "Shall we be sunder'd, shall we part, sweet girl?" she says.

"Never." I sling my arm around her waist. She pulls away and bats her false eyelashes at me. Why does she court me with words and looks, only to run away whenever I get close?

At lunch I go to the cafeteria to serve as Felicia's kitchen slave. But really I want to be part of the new daytime drama series—*Secrets and Lies and the People Who Tell Them*. My ulterior motives include a mother-daughter reconciliation. I know that I should repress thoughts like these, but they won't go away any more than my nervous mannerisms just because I tell them to. Besides, meddling could lead to a happy ending.

Felicia shows me the frozen vegetarian lasagna she plans to serve tomorrow.

"On behalf of all the bunny people at Yolo Bluffs High," I say, "thank you."

"You're welcome." Her smile contains less scary irony

than usual. The perfect time for the subtle opening I spent hours preparing has arrived.

"I know about Carmen," I say, "that she's your daughter."

Frailty, thy name is Roz. Translation? Bulldozers act with more subtle grace than I do.

Felicia looks angry. If eyes could chop vegetables, the carrots in front of her would be minced by now. She turns her back on me.

"She's very talented," I say. "You should be proud of her."

"I am proud of her," she says. "She's the one who's ashamed. And no wonder. You students treat us like maids."

Just like that, the chance of a lifetime waltzes into the kitchen on a platter (a terribly mixed metaphor, I know, but I'm that excited). Felicia confided in me. If I tell her that Carmen's a lesbian, I will save the two of them from years of misery.

"Did you know . . . that your daughter is in love with my sister?"

As much as I want to say it, I do NOT.

BigMouth to mission control—thank you for finding the impulse-control button in time. Inflammatory and indiscreet announcements are so last week for me. I'm still the same Roz, of course, but with an updated spam filter.

"I don't think of you that way," I say to Felicia instead. "And Carmen brags about you ALL the time." Okay, she brags about her pretend mom, but still. My new spam filter works to block uncomfortable truths. Friendly fibs can still slip through.

"I'll bet," Felicia says.

"Carmen's been doing an excellent job directing the play," I say to distract her. "She's a natural."

The crease between Felicia's lovely brows deepens. "She said she dropped out of the play."

Oops. There are still a few kinks in the system.

Just then BlueDragon gallops through the kitchen toward us. He slams into a plastic bucket and knocks it over. Frozen peas scatter across the floor. The qualities that the two of us share go way beyond questionable social skills. We both suffer from spastic body movements and bad timing, although I welcome the pandemonium right now. When I go to grab him, he slips out of my hands and leaps into a sink. It's full of water. Thoroughly panicked, he bounds out again and shakes water all over Felicia.

"Here, boy." Felicia waves a cooked chop in front of him. It must be something she brought from home because it doesn't resemble the mystery meat served at the cafeteria. BlueDragon inches toward the chop. When he gets the meat between his teeth, Felicia uses it as a kind of leash to drag him outside.

"Good work," I say.

My compliment fails to distract her.

"What's this about Carmen directing?"

"Well," I say to give myself time to invent a lie that is close enough to the truth to evade detection, "she dropped out of the play like you told her to. Only Sapphire begged her to direct this week because she would be away."

Gauging from Felicia's frown, few untruths slip past her. She strikes me as someone who missed a brilliant career as a spook.

"She promised to work on her scholarship essays after school."

"It's only for a few days," I beg. "The play will collapse

if she's not there to direct." I'm ready to offer anything. Like scrubbing the entire cafeteria floor. On my hands and knees. With a toothbrush. Carmen will kill me if she finds out I blabbed the truth to her mom. Slowly. And. Painfully. There has to be a way to undo my mistake.

Felicia notices my desperation. "Tough break," she says, consolingly.

"If you let her direct the play, I'll help her with her scholarship essays," I say.

"You," she scoffs. *Sinister violin music swells.* "Start by cleaning up this mess. When you finish, I'll think about it."

Chapter 20

I *miss fifth period* to chase down all the peas to Felicia's satisfaction. I slip in little hints as I work. For example, there is no reason she has to tell Carmen who ratted her out. Felicia plays impassive well, an effective foil to my pathetic grovel. I have the sense that I'm gliding backward on a conveyor belt. After a while I give up. To ensure that there will be witnesses when Carmen strangles me, I show up late to rehearsal. When I arrive, Eva isn't there, and Carmen looks happy—bordering on self-satisfied—so my betrayal is still a secret. For now.

The first scene on the rehearsal schedule won't be easy for Carmen. I wonder if she's nervous. She meets me in my manly disguise and falls into a deep passion for me. Though it's all pretend, she'll have to seduce an alleged lesbian (me) in front of everyone after working so hard to look heterosexual.

Carmen is not up to the challenge. Her attempt to swoon while praising me, "Sweet youth . . . I had rather hear you chide than this man woo," is a ghastly flop. She sounds like a girl cooing to an adorable baby bunny rather than flirting with the man she lusts after. And normally I'd tell her so in those exact words.

"Madam director?" I say instead. "I need to use the bathroom. Nico can fill in for me."

Nico fumbles through the script to find my next line. As I pass Andie below the stage, she grabs my wrist and appraises me.

"Where's the real Roz? And who the hell are you?"

"I'm just making nice like I said I would."

She lets go of my wrist. "Okay, but I'm watching you."

By the time I return, the cast has moved on to a scene I'm not in. Bryan looks like a hairball the cat coughed up. He drags himself through his lines with zombie-like tenacity. Maybe he's pining for me.

"He looks lovesick, don't you think?" I ask Andie.

"Men have died from time to time and worms have eaten them, but not for love," she replies. Translation? Boys are a lower life-form than worms.

I know what she means. For Bryan—as an example of a boy below worm level—the desire for sex trumps his need for a deeper connection. Girls are interested in fooling around too, but most want love to be a part of the equation. That makes girls choosier. I'm hoping my choosy side kicks in soon.

"Roz," Carmen calls out, "do you think Orlando should walk quickly cross-stage for this scene? The extra movement might enhance the illusion of anxiety."

She's thanking me for my timely bathroom break by asking for advice. I jump at the opportunity to be her assistant for the day. She treats me with respect for once, and I am careful not to touch her. By the end of rehearsal, we are a team. I find myself enjoying her ideas and her company despite our ugly past.

When Carmen dismisses everyone, Andie waves at me from a distance. "Got to go. See you," she shouts my way. She drags Nico with her. Our chummy threesome days are over.

Their departure gives me a few more friendly minutes with Madam Director before she goes home to the lion's den. I know what will happen after that. Felicia will yell at her for lying about the play, and Carmen will go back to hating me. I see now that we are twins in a way. We each play a role at school, trying to fake out the whole world about our identity.

"Want to go for coffee?" I ask, shocking us both.

"Another time, perchance?" she says.

After we part ways, I scoot to Yolo Bluffs' consignment shop and select a tight-fitting black dress with a scoop neckline. The dressing-room mirror talks to me when I try it on. Roz is a dish fit for the gods. Translation? I like myself today.

In the secrecy of my room, I cut out the back of the dress and sew two straps across like an X. After I've shredded the sleeves, added snaps around the neckline, and slit the skirt, the dress is perfect. My soft eyeliner pencil substitutes for black lipstick since the local drugstore failed to provide. I slather my eyes with outlandish eyeliner.

"Food!" Gethsemane yells through my door.

The look on her face—if I showed up in the kitchen dressed like this—would be worth a thousand laughs. I wash it all off. Long and misleading explanations about my appearance make for stressful dinner conversation. One scrubbed face and clothing change later, I finally make it to the table. Eva's seat is empty again.

"Has my sister joined the breathairians?" I ask. The breathairians claim to get all their nourishment from sunlight and fresh air.

"Ha ha. She caught a nasty bug," Mom says. "I want you to stay away from her."

"When's opening night?" Dad asks. He fills my plate. The spaghetti sauce has an odd texture to it.

"In ten days," I say. "We'll be rehearsing like crazy. Lucky for Eva she was born reciting Shakespeare. She'll catch up."

It turns out that tofu does not go well with marinara. I feel bad that Dad and Mom have to eat it too. Let's just say that no one pigs out tonight.

After jamming the red-smeared plates into the dishwasher, I obey Mom's edict to leave Eva alone. More or less. I can't catch the flu spying through her bedroom window, right? And the universe grants me a boon. There's a wedge-shaped gap where she didn't close the curtain all the way. I watch her kneeling on the floor and whispering. Maybe she's rehearsing for a scene in the play. She leaps to her feet and waltzes a pillow around the room.

The next morning, I enter homeroom with fear in my heart. When Carmen smiles at me, I know that Felicia has granted me a second reprieve. But for how long? Eyeliner

Andie distracts me from my worries with her style du jour. Her cheeks are contoured with blue blush—if you can call blue powder blush—and her pigtails have been moussed into insect antennae. She's holding hands with Nico, who has a fat rubber band around his wrist like a bracelet. This must be part of her scheme.

"Everyone quiet for announcements," Mr. Beltz says.

When Nico whispers to me, "I don't believe in announcements," Andie snaps his rubber band. "Ow," he says.

Andie puts her notebook in her lap, scribbles on it and tilts it toward me.

Jonathan survived the visit with parents so far.

I flash her a "great news" smile. Though the news IS great, jealousy interferes with my happiness. Jonathan used to be my friend, whereas he and Andie barely know each other. Why did he tell her and not me? True, their characters fall in love and get married in the play, but off-stage they're practically strangers. Why am I always the last to know every single significant thing? Maybe the TV commercials are right. Everything would change for the better if I just switched brands of deodorant.

Me (quill in hand): is he coming back?
Her: yes
Me: great!
Her: great for us, sad for him
Me: poor J
Her: sigh
Me: coming to my house to rehearse after school?
Her: yes *smiles to show large teeth*

At lunch I take the chance to worm into Felicia's good graces by actually volunteering to feed the dishwasher—a device like a mini carwash—a chore I've done only once before when she ordered me to. Women pay top dollar for spa treatments like this, I tell myself as the steam from the boiling water lays open my pores. My hard work catches Felicia's attention.

"You're stacking the trays too high."

"Sorry," I say. "Have you decided? About the play?"

The sparkle in her eyes softens from diamond to granite.

"A health inspector will be by tomorrow. I'm organizing a cleaning party for tonight. Seven P.M. to midnight."

The line between opportunity and threat can blur. "See you there," I say.

When I slip out the back entrance of the cafeteria while rubbing lotion into my poor chapped hands, Bryan jumps out from behind a stack of boxes and pulls me against him. His breath warms my ear, and my neck skin begs for his lips. I yell at my body to behave itself, but it refuses to obey.

"You to my love must accord, or have a woman for your lord," he says. Translation? He wants to lord it over ME.

"Lordette," I say.

"I broke up with Eva," he says.

I wriggle out of his arms. "You're such a player. She broke up with *you*."

"Because she knew I was about to break up with her," he says, kissing my palm. "Girls like it when you give them the power."

I have relived each moment in the peach orchard with

Bryan without my golden lenses and soft-focus delusions. Multiple times. Despite the ugly events of that day, I can't purge him from my system. I hate that in a boy. He's worse than static cling. I push back the sleeves of my top. My body-art has faded in the shower, but he can still read it.

He kisses the soft underside of my forearm where the letters are the clearest. "See, I'm right. You care about me."

I yank my hand away from him. "I cared. Past tense," I say. "Until the veils were lifted." Thankfully, he can't hear the pounding of my traitorous heart.

After school I zip home to don my new black dress and freaky makeup. RoZ goeZ Goth. My parents went to a music event in Sacramento. I have the house to myself. Except for the ghost girl in room two, but she's not likely to come out from her compound to interfere with my plans. The black-leather studded wristband I bought turns out to be big, so I turn it into a collar for Marshmallow. Should I add a leash to the ensemble?

When Andie arrives, she gives me the once-over.

"You look different somehow," she says.

"You said you're into Goth girls," I say.

"The writing on your legs is original. A new kind of mesh stocking?" She removes a little pipe from her purse and packs it carefully with marijuana. "Do you mind?"

"By the window," I say.

She hangs her head outside to exhale, and the smoke from her mouth mingles with the fog. She offers the pipe to me.

"No, thanks," I say. "My grandma died of lung cancer."

"From smoking pot?"

"It gives me a headache."

She takes a second hit and passes the pipe to me more forcefully this time. I inhale so she'll stop acting like a pest. After a few more tokes between us, she stashes the pipe in her bag, squirts a blast of air-freshener into my room, and offers me a mint. "That's better," she says.

Marshmallow curls up in my lap, shedding hair onto my dress. I'm guessing Goths don't have white cats for a reason. I push her off me and ramp up a playlist I burned earlier.

"Do you like the Butchies?" I ask.

Andie giggles. "Never heard of them."

I laugh too. "They sound butch," I say.

The song goes "*caught in an ice storm, caught in your eyes, and I'm losing my mind, but I'm winning you.*" Andie's eyes are rimmed with a wide swath of shimmery copper, outlined in dark blue, with a curved end-point like a belly dancer's. We are lying next to each other on my bed almost touching. The colorful fish in my mobile blend into one another. I roll onto my side and look into her eyes.

"Can I kiss you?" I ask.

"Looking for lesbian cred?" she says.

"What?"

"I know you're faking it."

I roll onto my back away from her. "You do?"

"Not on purpose, maybe. It could be that you've faked yourself out. Either way, your vibe isn't right." Andie leans back on her elbows. "I have this theory about you."

"Oh yeah," I say. I'm the one with the clever theories. Her having a theory about me makes me nervous.

"You're only attracted to the unavailable."

This surprises me so much I forget to be mad. Could it

be true? My past crushes and boyfriends parade through my mind, doing the long runway walk you see in fashion shows. I consider each one in turn. Andie's theory *would* explain my short-lived interest in Eva's ex-boyfriends. And in the seventh grade I flirted obsessively with a cute bagger at the supermarket, a high school student with his ear pierced in a dozen places. When bagger-guy kissed me behind a wall of sodas one day, he turned into a sucker-fish. I didn't go back to the store for six months.

And my obsession with Andie fits the theory like a Lycra tank top, hugging every curve. I pursue her only when she makes it clear that she's not into me. I want what I can't have. Worse still, I don't want what I CAN have. And worst of all, I don't know what I want.

"You might be right about me," I say. "Can I kiss you anyway?"

Her face gives me no clues to her feelings. "Yes," she says.

Chapter 21

She said yes. When I breathe in, the straps of my dress pull tight across my back and clamp my rib cage. I hear the threatening ping of stitches giving way. Eva could barge in on us at any time. The black "lipstick" cracks on my lower lip. I smooth it with my finger.

"But you have to promise me something first," she says.

"Okay, what?"

"I won't tell you what it is. But you have to promise anyway. I'll collect later."

Classic Andie. She could ask for anything—a promise not to tell, a promise to tell everything, or a vacation for two on the Island of Lesbos.

"I promise," I say.

"That style looks good on you," she says.

I keep my breaths small on account of the dress and gaze into her eyes until the little flecks of green make me dizzy. "It is the east, and Andie is the sun." Translation? However crazy the circumstances, and no matter how strange this feels, I'm a hopeless romantic through and through. If only Bryan had tried that line on me.

She keeps her eyes open as I close the distance

between us. I let our lips touch before moving to her lower lip. She kisses my upper lip, and I stop breathing entirely. I can't tell if my heart palpitations are from nervousness or excitement. Marshmallow jumps onto the bed, climbs over me, and wedges herself in the tiny space between my body and Andie's. I ignore her plaintive mew because I'm concentrating on what to do with my tongue. Before I figure it out, Andie pulls back laughing.

"What's wrong?"

"It's funny, that's all." She scratches Marshmallow between the ears and then reaches across my cat to brush a tendril of hair off my cheek. "Since you're so into labels . . . ," she begins, "if I had to label myself . . . I'd call myself a no-sexual."

The song ends, and I jump off the bed to stop the music before the next lesbian love ballad begins. Vigorous physical action provides a good cover for feelings, whatever my feelings may be—rejection, relief, uncertainty, or some combination of the three.

"I like you," she says. "Like like. But I'm not that big into physical expression."

My next intake of breath pops a few more stitches. One kiss didn't provide any big answers to my questions. I decide then and there that uncertainty is a good thing. I'll call myself a maybe-perhaps-a-little-bit bisexual. Either that or I was a lesbian in a past life and my current life is the echo.

When Nico arrives, Andie hangs on to his arm like he's her favorite exhibit in the Weird Boys Hall of Fame, a lot of touching for a girl who's not that physical. Nico avoids looking at me. I feel like the Medusa until I catch him peeking at my bodice, which is literally bursting at the seams. Apparently ogling below the chin doesn't turn a person to stone. After running through three scenes, the pounding techno-funk headache I predicted becomes reality. I kick both of them out.

I pace from room to room around the house. If only Eva would come out of her tomb, my dress could spark a conversation between us. At dinnertime I graze on leftovers from the refrigerator. Goth types strike me as flesh-eaters, and that's how I justify munching down a cold breakfast sausage and half a pork burrito. After dinner I change into some old sweats for my cleaning date at the cafeteria. Wardrobe is everything. I could be the star of a modern Cinderella story in reverse. Except I'm meeting a scary woman half my height instead of a prince. Oh well.

When I get there, Felicia greets me with a bucket and a scrub brush. She assigns me to an oversized oven. My arms get sore just looking at it.

"Directing a play gives you management experience," I say.

"You never give up, do you?" Felicia says. "Carmen is my family. I want the best for her."

"Exactly," I say.

I'll wear her down with elbow grease. The inside of the oven is coated with black gunk. Hard work gives a person time to reflect. Now that my head is clear, I think way, way back to the events that led up to this afternoon. True, faking my sexuality on a dare could be seen as shallow. Some might say shallower than a pond in a drought. But I had other reasons. I thought that my coming-out would create a new bond with Eva, a shared experience. In retrospect that reason was dumb, though not exactly shallow. Some people go to Europe to broaden themselves. I just took an alternate route. Inventing a girlfriend let me explore new lands, make new friends, and learn a few things, all without the expensive airline ticket.

Just at the moment I start feeling pretty good about myself despite the fumes from the oven cleaner and the crick in my neck, I hear a voice that sends shivers down my spine. Carmen. Maybe if I work on the back wall of the oven, she won't spot me.

"What are you doing here?"

Pixie butts are inconspicuous. Amazon butts are not. I emerge from the oven and baby-step in her direction to give myself time to think. Unfortunately, I wouldn't be able to explain away my presence if I had a hundred years to think up a good lie. Felicia stands at Carmen's side with her arms crossed over her chest.

"Helping," I say.

"She thinks if she gets on my good side, I'll let you stay in the play," Felicia says.

I risk a quick look at Carmen. Her color is high, but I can't tell anything from the strange expression on her face.

"And it's working," I say boldly.

"Maybe," Felicia says. "I'll tell you after the third oven is spotless." She dismisses me with a wave of her hand, and I go back to my post. Scrubbing off stubborn grease turns out to be great for channeling nervous energy. I stop now and then to rest my sore muscles and check on Carmen's whereabouts. She leaves before I can get her alone. Eons later, I present my three shiny ovens to Felicia.

"You can go home now," she says. In Felicia-speak this means that I won. I refrain from expressing jubilation until I get outside.

When Eva doesn't come out of her room for breakfast on Thursday morning, I put a cup to the wall between us. She's been languishing from fake-out flu for three days now, setting a new Peterson record. I know all the tricks from years of experience. Warm the thermometer to 102 on your computer. Rub the bottom of your nose vigorously to redden it. Leave crumpled tissues scattered about on the floor. Moisten your face. Crying lends authenticity to the look, but a wet washcloth will do in a pinch.

I hear a drawer in her room scraping open. She says, "I'm not feeling well," several times, each version more clogged up than the last. After a short silence, she says, "Hey, Carmen. I won't be at rehearsal. I'm still not feeling well. Sorry."

So I'll be facing Madam Director today on my own. I've already chewed my nails to their nubs. Just as I'm about to stop spying on Eva to better chew on my sleeve, she speaks aloud again. This time her voice projects with vigor and emotion.

"To you I give myself, for I am yours."

I drop the cup and succumb to a full-blown freak-out, a quiet one, involving much chest clutching and rolling around on my rug. I ball my hands into fists to protect my nail nubs from my teeth. Eva's holed up in her room rehearsing Rosalind's lines. My lines. She means to steal the lead from me somehow. I need Andie. Now. She will think of something to avert a total nervous breakdown. But her cell is turned off.

When I charge into homeroom—out of breath and sweaty from maniacal scooting fueled by outrage—the first thing I see is Andie's empty seat snuggled up to Nico's empty seat. As the minutes dribble past, the truth dawns on me. She and Nico ditched homeroom without inviting me. I could summon her by telekinesis, except I'm more psycho than psychic. Carmen's seat is empty too, so really I should be thankful. I sit on my hands, pretend my feet are nailed down to avoid unseemly knee bouncing, and gnash my teeth as quietly as possible until the bell rings.

Andie shows up at rehearsal flushed and happy. Nico trails three feet behind her. He's her new pet iguana trained to heel. Carmen has yet to arrive, and I breathe a sigh of relief.

"Where were you today? I needed to ask you something," I say to Andie.

Nico hangs out next to her with his back toward me, which looks pretty weird, to be honest. What's his freaking deal? First he stalks me and now he ignores me. More than ignores me. Shuns me.

"I'll grant you three questions," Andie says with a bow. I swear she's part genie and part Sphinx. "Choose carefully."

"Girl talk," I say to Nico, swatting him away. "Leave us." He stumbles twice in his hurry to get away.

"Were you getting physical with Nico this morning?"

"Wrong question," she says.

That has to mean yes. I decide not to dwell on how this

makes me feel. "I overheard Eva rehearsing Rosalind's lines. Do you think she has a plan up her sleeve to off me so she can play Rosalind on opening night?"

"That's way outside the AndieZone. You'll have to ask her yourself. Last question."

"But you haven't even answered ONE."

"It's not my fault you're wasting them like a fool in a fairy tale."

"Why has Nico stopped liking me?"

Andie flashes her International Woman of Mystery smile. "Because I told him to." She makes to walk toward the stage, but I block her path.

"Did you tell him to like me in the first place?"

She taps my temple gently with her yin-yang-painted nail. "Hello? Anybody home?"

Carmen arrives and calls us to begin. I'm nervous in her presence because I can't predict what she'll do to me. She has to be furious that I revealed her secret involvement in the play to her mother. But she also knows I went to great lengths to make up for it. And I know a secret about her she doesn't want out. In fact, she won't breathe the word *cafeteria* around me for the rest of the school year. But she could try something more subtle. Like pricking me with her poisoned hairpin.

We rehearse the final scenes of the play, where everyone has fallen in love with someone who's fallen in love with someone else. Romantic entanglements haven't changed much in the last several centuries. Downtrodden shepherd Nico loves haughty shepherdess Carmen, but Carmen loves me disguised as a man. Bryan pretends to woo the mannish version of me, but loves the absent womanish me instead. Despite all the confusion, I promise all will marry on the morrow. I lose myself in the scene.

Nico slumps his shoulders and says, "Love is to be all made of sighs and tears; and so am I for Phebe."

Carmen makes doe eyes at me. "And I for Ganymede."

Bryan drops to his knees and grasps my masculine hand. "And I for Rosalind."

I adopt Andie's impossible-to-read smile. "And I for no woman," I say.

Bryan's burning looks promise future passion of the backseat variety, and I let myself enjoy the fantasy. It distracts me from my other worries. His constant wooing—the sad puppy eyes and brows teaming up to beg for my love—gratifies me after so many months of longing for him. Then again, now that he's abundantly available, his platinum glow fails to blind me to the same degree. Is Andie right that I want only what I can't have? Or maybe I've finally recognized the real Bryan, not the guy he plays on TV.

When we finish practicing our bows, Carmen asks me to stay after. I hate unrehearsed death scenes, but I can't think up an excuse to leave.

"Who knew you had that kind of talent?" I say the second we are alone.

She blushes, but I detect hostility beneath the profusion of pink. I quickly pluck a tissue from my bag and wave it like a surrender flag.

"Can't we be friends?" I say.

"How long have you known about my mom?" She picks up the broom and does a frantic sweeping thing with it.

"A few days, but I haven't told anyone. Not even Eva."

"Why not? You usually blab everything."

She should be thanking me for my discretion, kowtowing to my feet, offering to massage them. In scented oil. Three times a day.

"I've turned over a new leaf," I say. I cough a little from the dust she's stirring up.

"But you told my mom I was directing the play."

It's my turn to pretend sweeping. I snatch the broom away and hand her my surrender flag. "Not on purpose. It just slipped out." I hide in my cloud of dust waiting for the prick of death. When it doesn't come, I keep on talking. "Your mom really cares about you. My mom hardly notices me."

"Want to trade?"

I think about Mom in SuperMode—faster than a speeding bullet. But Felicia can leap tall buildings in a single bound and would squash her like a bug.

"I'll pass," I say. "Not much gets by Felicia. That's a quality I don't need in a mom."

Carmen blows her nose in my surrender flag. I take it as a sign that our feud is over. We've become the keepers of each other's secrets.

"I've got to go," I say.

"Can I ask you something first?" Carmen says. "Why hasn't Eva shown her face at rehearsals? Is she really sick?"

"No," I say. "She's been hiding in her room practicing Rosalind's part. I think she plans to steal the role from me."

"No way." She hesitates for a moment. "I might try that, but Eva? She would never stoop that low. Don't you know her at all?"

I do, actually. Despite Eva's imperfections, her feet barely reach the ground.

Home suffers from unearthly quiet. The parents are still at work, and Eva has become a hermit. I turn on my computer for company. Electronic messages are solace for the lonely. Among the spam, unread horoscopes, and unsigned petitions, two gems await me in my inbox. I read the email from Sierra first.

hey girlfriend
i loved hearing your news, well except for the troubles with eva. lezzie roz made me laugh so hard i got a stomachache AND peed my pants. i crazy time miss you. breaking glass means bad juju btw. something in your life has gotten out of whack. i threw some cards and they said be yourself.
i love u . . . but not like that you perv ;) !!!!
xoxoxoxoxoxoxoxoxoxo S

I read her message over and over like a hundred times. It's a relief she thinks I should be myself. But then again who is that? And maybe I should be 98 percent Roz instead of 100 percent. Drop the 2 percent that wants to tell Felicia that Carmen prefers girls. Tact can be a good thing once in a while. Not to mention staying out of other people's business occasionally. I read the email from Jonathan next.

pixie
i read that coming out story u gave me . . . mine went nothing like that . . . lol. . . .
i told a friend . . . he spread it around . . . my girlfriend broke up with me. . . .

2 boyz tried to beat me up . . . teacher broke up the
fight. . . .
i told my mom who told my dad. . . .
they sent me to our church . . . when that didn't
work . . . they called Aunt S. . . .
the rest is history. . . .
my dad doesn't want me in the house until i'm
cured. . . .
back on monday
pyro

All the messy tears I've stuffed away into my basement over the years come pouring out after I read it. Parents are supposed to accept their children no matter what—tend their autistic offspring, love their ugly losers, and defend their murderer sons on death row. Jonathan is OH-SO lovable. I will never judge a person who keeps his or her sexuality private. Not anymore, anyway. When I get a grip on myself, I reply to his email.

to thine own self be true. your friends here love the
real you.

I've become part of something bigger after all. It hurts more than I expected. The soulful tune playing on my stereo blends with the mixed-up feelings tumbling around inside me. Everything that's happened in the last few weeks comes into focus. Not that I understand it better. I am sure that Jonathan is my friend, though. He's seen my dark side, and he still cares about me. There should be a word for that.

I dry my tears. Too bad I forgot to ask Sierra for advice

on my love life. Of course, the pertinent details change more often than the daily special at a sidewalk bistro. Now that Nico and Andie have glommed into a bizarre unit that could be called a couple and Eva broke up with Bryan for real, should I go for him? I want to have someone to call my own. Despite his bad behavior he has this bizarre effect on me. I can't entirely eliminate him from my system, type "format H," and reboot my heart.

Thus the Bryan voodoo doll is born. A few socks, the blond hair from my old Barbie, a little twine, a magic marker, and voilà, mini Bryan. Sierra would be so proud. First he woos me. *Goddess sweet and yet divine, such a girl is Rosalind, etc.* Then I slap him around some and make him kiss my unwashed feet. Voodoo doll Bryan has eyes only for me.

Eva fails to show for rehearsal on Friday, and this is worrying. Her mental health day has stretched into a week. She won't answer the taps on her door or the notes I've pasted to her window. Opening night is a mere week away. She could be suffering from PTBS (Post Traumatic Bryan Syndrome). Or is this about my lesbian act at school? In any case, I have no doubt I am to blame somehow.

Andie and Nico keep on treating me like I'm barely there, without the decency even to notice me ignoring them in return. RoZ iZ despiZed. Just days ago Andie said she liked me. And Nico defended me when Bryan called me a dyke. He laughed at my jokes. Okay, so he also ate what looked like a gift from BlueDragon in front of all the theater geeks. Still, he looks good with Andie's waif arms around his torso.

"Should the couples be seated or standing whilst they

await your arrival?" Carmen asks me. Luckily for my ever-shrinking ego, now flea-sized and in danger of vanishing altogether, Carmen has asked me to sit with her in homeroom again. And she consults me constantly during rehearsals.

"Standing," I say. "That shows their anticipation."

She jots a note on her script and calls for some chairs. She makes me feel as if we're doing this together, that I'm her codirector. I return the favor by taking her side in arguments and complimenting her ideas. When we finish, she says, "Are you going to the Silo, perchance?"

"What? By myself?"

"With me," she says. The idea of Carmen as my actual friend has yet to take root. It rotates around my consciousness like when BlueDragon circles a spot on the grass. A person wonders if he will actually lie down before the lunch minute is over.

"Let's go," I say. She bikes slowly alongside my scooter.

"Sorry," she says, pointing her chin at the DykeByke graffiti.

"Sorry." I nod at the bald spot on her frame. I wonder if she's going to apologize for the threatening alien sign. She doesn't.

When we get to the Silo, she stands at the counter to order while I settle us at a table. "My notes are in the side pocket of my bag," she says.

I'm hungry, but a muffin at the Silo costs a small fortune. You'd think they were made from beluga caviar and gold dust. So I unzip the top of her sports duffel to search for free snacks.

"I said the pocket!" Carmen yells. As she sprints

toward me, I stop going through her things to look at her. Wherefore the sudden panic?

"Any munchies in here?" I hold up a plastic grocery bag.

She snatches it away from me and it rips open, scattering a hundred gum wrappers onto the floor. Juicy Fruit gum wrappers, to be precise.

Chapter 22

I watch Carmen as she stoops to sweep up the gum wrappers. Top-quality acting is always worth observing. The clenched expression on her face changes to bewilderment. I anticipate her accompanying lines. *Where did these come from? I never saw them in my life.* Or, *Is there a law against chewing gum?* But the inexplicable happens. Tears spring to her eyes as she lets the wrappers slip through her fingers onto our table like dirt onto a coffin in an open grave. Okay, I've never seen a coffin in an open grave, but her face does say mournful.

I help her along. "You're the Peeping Tom," I say.

"WE are. Were. It was Eva's idea." She flattens one of the wrappers using the edge of the table. "The Birkenstocks too. When we were . . . friends."

What is this—National Confession Week? I didn't spike her coffee with truth serum. I swear.

"Wow," I say.

"You know how tedious it can be around here. We'd look into windows, scatter gum wrappers, and try not to laugh too loudly."

"Did you ever see anything . . . interesting?"

"You wouldn't believe how many people pick their noses when they think no one is watching. Once we saw Mr. Duncan with his hands down his pants. I thought I'd die. We never went back." She blushes and looks down at the tabletop.

"Weren't you afraid of getting caught?" I ask.

"Not really. We'd go to houses with the TV blaring." She takes a sip of coffee. "Promise you won't tell anyone. Police officers have no sense of humor. And my mom less than that."

"I promise."

When Carmen smiles, I feel good that she trusts me. BlueDragon finishes circling and settles down for a nap. We have become friends.

On Saturday morning I make myself quinoa hot cereal for breakfast with chopped nuts, soy milk, and a distinct lack of syrup. If this weren't bad enough, Mom comes in and frowns at me. "You did something to upset Eva," she says.

Is she referring to my secret date with Bryan? Or snagging the lead in the play maybe? But I thought Eva had broken up with him, and I can't be blamed for acting well. Oh, there's that other little thing—coming out as a lesbian at school.

"No," I say.

Mom gives me a look. She's been using that ESP of hers again. "An apology is worth a thousand words," she says. "You should talk to her. She's not contagious anymore."

"Fine. But you'll have to make her let me in first," I say. "Her door is barricaded."

Mom goes to Eva's room and taps lightly. When there's no answer, I say, "See?"

"It's Mom. Roz has something she'd like to say to you."

Eva opens the door right away.

"All you had to do was knock," Gethsemane says.

"I have a surprise for you," I say. "Just wait here." I dash to my room, retrieve a certain something, and return with it tucked under my shirt. Mom has retreated to give us privacy. I lock Eva's door behind me just in case.

"You're pregnant?" Eva asks.

"Ta da!" I whip it out. "A Bryan voodoo doll. You can work out your aggressions on it."

Eva studies the lumpy socks and patchy hair. "Looks like someone worked him over pretty well already."

Now comes the hard part, the part where years of acting can be nifty because I don't exactly mean what I'm about to say. I adjust an earring and nibble delicately on my pinkie nail. "I'm sorry I flirted with your boyfriend." I stare at a spot on the wall before shifting my gaze to the floor.

Eva laughs, a startling sound to be sure. "You were crushing on him first. I knew that before we hooked up."

I drop the act. "You did?" Who knew the depths of her depravity?

"It was pretty obvious."

"Did you even like him?"

"Of course. He's a sexy beast. Just the right sort of devil to help me get over my breakup with Brad Pitt."

I tackle her and pin her to the bed. *"Folly-fallen scullion,"* I say, trying to get my fingers around her neck.

She slides out of my grip. "It started out as payback, Chub. You know, for Marcus and John and—"

"Stop," I say. According to my memory banks, I pursued only TWO of her ex-boyfriends. If there were more, I don't want to know. "And don't call me Chub."

"What *should* I call you?"

"Slim," I say. I pick up the Bryan doll from the floor. I might have future use for it. "Since you don't want him . . . may I?"

Eva laughs so hard it's contagious, and we run around her room shrieking and throwing things like we used to. Soon I'm lying on the floor covered in socks, pillows, and stray sweaters trying to catch my breath. As the last convulsive giggle leaves my chest, I look at Eva sitting next to me. Her hair is tousled, and she looks twelve years old.

"Why did you lie to me when you got your period?" I ask.

"I lied?"

"I found tampons in your room, and you said they were for cleaning your ears."

"Oh, that. I guess I thought it would mean a lot to you to be first."

I go a tad gooey when she says that. The days when she looked out for me were sweet. Maybe if I give her what she wants most, I can bring them back. "Are you still mad I got the lead?" I say.

"Obviously you bribed Sapphire for the role. But what I want to know is how you got your hands on a million dollars."

"Ha! I earned it fair and square," I say. "But you can have it. It's yours." My offer comes out through gritted teeth and doesn't sound as gracious as I planned.

"Roz?" Eva says. She folds me into a long hug. "You

really do love me." When she lets go, her eyes are wet. "I can't believe what you just said. But that's not what I want."

"I don't understand. I heard you rehearsing my lines in here."

She wipes her face on her sleeve. "I wasn't rehearsing for the play."

"What were you rehearsing for?"

"Nothing."

"This nothing that you so plentifully give me," I say. Translation? She will never open up to me. They say you learn more from your failures than your successes. Well, I learned something today. Failure sucks.

I pace her room, stopping to fluff a pom-pom here and straighten a trophy there. "Okay, okay! I'm sorry," I say, not acting this time, except to control the excesses of my jumpy body parts. "I'm sorry I came out at school."

Like superglue, she hardens in seconds. "What were you thinking?"

What WAS I thinking?

"I didn't mean to offend anyone," I say. "I wanted to join a cool club, I guess. And to show you that people are more tolerant than you think."

"Tolerant? Like you?" She picks up her foot behind her back and stretches her quad.

"What do you mean by that?"

"Who wants to be tolerated, anyway?" She holds her arms out and rotates them in small circles. "I want to be accepted. People who can't accept others don't love themselves."

"I love myself," I say. With a few reservations. I can see

it now, the worst-selling self-help book of all time—*I Love Myself . . . Almost*.

"Good for you." She bends over to stretch her hamstrings, resting her palms on the floor and making it look easy. "Only it's not always about you."

What are we talking about exactly?

Eva's cell phone rings, Pachelbel's Sappiest Canon. She pushes me out the door before answering it.

Chapter 23

Eva skips yet another day of school. I envy my sister her strange powers over Gethsemane and Elmo. Now that I have friends, though, I look forward to going to school. And I wouldn't miss today in exchange for a future Emmy. Jonathan will be back, and I mean to drag him off into a corner of the Barn to lavish him with love (Platonic, of course). Our new friendship means a lot to me.

At rehearsal Carmen foils my plan by whisking him onto the stage to work through the scenes we postponed during his abduction. Despite his haunted look, he moves across the stage without stumbling over wires or half-remembered lines. I should get his autograph before he becomes famous. Not to sell, either, but as proof that he knew me before he had a shelf lined with Tony Awards.

When Sapphire comes in, I intercept her. "Watch Carmen a minute before you go up there," I whisper.

As we observe together, Carmen listens to suggestions from the other players and makes decisions with quiet authority, so unlike her usual bossy mode. She maneuvers the scene off its lazy backside and ratchets the tension into high gear.

"Oh, my," Sapphire says.

"Yes," I say. "You should let her finish out the week." It feels good to put my slithery serpent mind to a less selfish use for once.

"Good idea."

Sapphire seems cheerful about this, so I risk a second good deed. "How did it go?"

"How did what go?"

"Will Jonathan's parents take him back?" I ask.

"He told you about his parents?"

"I think they're horrible," I say.

Sapphire crosses her arms tight and scrunches her shoulders. "That's my sister you're talking about," she says.

At that moment, I remember how Sapphire called Jonathan confused, and the piranha inside me slips her leash. "That's no excuse to treat him like a criminal."

"Don't be so dramatic. They didn't lock him up," she says. "But he's making a choice that hurts them."

I have trouble keeping my voice down. "What about hurting him? Why would he CHOOSE to be gay if it's so much easier not to be? How can you believe that?"

"Teens are often self-destructive, and feelings aren't always logical," she says. "You'll understand when you're a mother."

My anger builds to violence, the hair-pulling, nail-scratching, and shin-kicking kind. I storm off to stew behind the speaker. When I have a daughter a million years from now, I will accept her for who she is. More than that, I will encourage her to follow her heart, to embrace herself. I hope she turns out to be even crazier than I am.

During the break, Sapphire talks to Carmen. When Andie drags Nico behind the props, I ask Jonathan to take a breath of air with me.

"You still remember your lines," I say.

"Pretty much. But I can't stop thinking about my mom. She wants me back, but Dad says no. And she's going along with it. It's insane."

"Since you go both ways, couldn't you . . . you know . . . ?" As soon as the idea takes shape in my head and right before the last few words enter the air in front of my mouth, I know how wrong I am. I should sell my big mouth on eBay under Blooper Collectibles. "Forget I said that." I clap a hand over my mouth to emphasize the point. "To thine own self be true."

"Huh, what?" he asks from Jonathan Land. He gently pulls my hand away from my mouth. It appears that he missed my faux pas. Thank the goddess for small blessings. He squeezes my hand so that the bones crunch into each other. "Thanks."

"You're way ahead of all the gays in the closet," I say. "It's good to be out and proud. Strength in numbers."

"Tell that to Matthew Shepard."

I try to wriggle my fingers. "Who?"

"Don't give me that shit," he says.

When I get home, Dad surprises me in the kitchen. We make tomato-garlic soup with heaps of onion and squash, performing each task as if for an haute cuisine show on TV. I use a fake Italian accent as a foil to his fake French accent. For a while I can pretend that everything is back to normal, that Sierra still lives in Yolo Bluffs, Eva still loves me, and everyone takes my obsession with boys for granted. Ah, the simple life.

"Zee squash shood be tendair," he says, holding out his pinkie finger as he jabs at the zucchini with a fork.

"Coat da garlick wit da oil olivo. Perfetto," I say, drizzling the yellow-green oil into the pan. We kiss our fingertips after each step. Just when I'm feeling especially happy, Elmo fixes me with one of those long, uncomfortable stares of his.

"What?" I say, drilling him back with my cyborg eye.

"I love both my daughters, whatever happens."

"I'll hold you to that," I say in a tough voice—though I'm going all squishy inside—"when I embark on my new career."

"Which career is that?"

"Serial ax murderer."

After dinner I hit the Google. Matthew Shepard was a gay college student living in Laramie, Wyoming. One night he was hanging out in a bar when two young guys offered him a ride home. They drove him to a remote spot, tied him to a fence, and beat him. He wasn't found until the next day. A few days after that, he died while still in a coma. Later in court, the young men claimed he was hitting on them. No wonder I spend so much time in my invented life. Nothing that horrible ever happens there. Sometimes reality sucks more than I can handle.

I make an altar to Matthew using a photo printed off the Net and illuminating it with a scented candle Sierra gave me. I write his name on the skin near my heart. I download an uplifting coming-out story to cheer myself up, reading it through a haze of sandalwood.

> My name is Jay. Like a lot of boys in the third grade, I had a crush on my teacher. Only my teacher was a man. I kept it to myself. Then the whole story poured out of me unexpectedly at my fifteenth birthday party. My friends were upset with me, but not because I was gay. They were mad I hadn't trusted them to support me. Though it was the happiest day of my life, I couldn't stop crying.

I visit a Christian Web site that says God won't punish gays unless they consummate their love with physical acts. So gays are supposed to remain celibate? Like that could ever work for anyone with hormones. Except for the no-sexuals, I guess. I forward Jay's coming-out story to them and to Sapphire while I'm at it.

Tuesday morning Andie shows up in homeroom for the first time in many days sans pet. The combination of white makeup and a red-streaked scarf wrapped around her neck like a blood-soaked bandage gives her a positively ghoulish look. If I kiss her cheek, will her head topple and roll across the floor?

"Where's Nico?" I ask.

She sets a stack of date-stamped photos on the table in front of me. As I leaf through them, a pattern emerges—Bryan holding hands with a girl, Bryan kissing a girl, and Bryan fondling the butt of a girl. The theme of each picture is the same, but the girl is not. All the while that Bryan has been giving me the woo, he's been hooking up with two freshman girls on the side. *Eye-offending, wenching rampallion.* The girls are shorter and skinnier than I am. But let's not forget what we have in common. Stupidity.

Andie offers me a tissue from her funereal black purse.

"Yesterday's news," I say. "Who took the pictures?"

"Nico."

"Why?" I ask.

"Do I have to spell out everything for you? You're not in kindergarten anymore."

"He's *your* boyfriend."

She rolls her eyes so vigorously, it's a wonder they don't fall out of their sockets.

The afternoon of our first dress rehearsal, we sift through gowns and petticoats in a curtained-off dressing area called the Mosh Pit. I turn toward the wall when I take off my shirt, but despite the evasion, Andie spots the ballpoint tattoo on my clavicle.

"That's passion." She traces the name with her finger. "New boyfriend?"

By her smile I can tell she knows about Matthew Shepard. "We met at a séance," I say. "He's perfect for me. He doesn't fool around with other girls, and he always compliments me on what I'm wearing."

She zips my dress, and we both stare at the vision I make in the mirror. Now that she doesn't want to get physical with me, I can enjoy her appreciative looks with palpitations minus the panic. I straighten my shoulders from their usual slump that helps me feel shorter.

"I hear him paying you a compliment right now," she says.

Mirrors don't lie. The fitted bodice, puffed sleeves, and

A-line skirt transform me from giantess to goddess. I could slay the heart of Zeus himself. And Juno's, too.

After rehearsal, I add a dried red rose and a Lindor truffle to Matthew's altar. Who knew he'd become my closest confidant? Not really, but I've talked to him more than anybody else today. Ever since I offered Eva the world, apologized for everything, even the parts that weren't my fault, she's blown frosty air my way. She doesn't want Bryan anymore. She doesn't want the lead in the play. There must be an explanation for why she's hibernating in her room. *It's not always about you,* she said.

Talk to me, talk to me, talk to me, I plead to the wall between us. Sierra said the broken glass means that some part of my life is out of whack. And that part is this strange disconnect between Eva and me. But I don't know how to cast off the bad juju. How do I get my sister back?

Soon she'll dance off to college, start a career in a distant city, get married to someone I can't stand, have sticky babies, and send me a lousy e-card once a year on my birthday. I should go to her room right now and shake her till she talks. My favorite Ouija Web site might tell me what to do. As I type *why,* a banner slides across my screen, a ghostly answer to my prayers.

I'm in love with Carmen. Will you help me Slim?

I banner her back. *YES!!!!*

Chapter 24

I knew it, I knew it, and I knew it some more. I'm not as delusional as everyone gives me credit for. But when I throw myself through Eva's door—after her banner we're so beyond knocking—she's not there. I search under the bed and behind the curtains. Her cell is off too. That's just as well because answering my thousand and one questions will take more minutes than her plan can handle. Where is she?

I hop on one foot and deny my teeth the food they crave—my new fingernail extensions painted to look like miniature zebras. After that I go to the office to ask Mom.

"Where's Eva?" I say as if it doesn't matter.

She looks up from her work. "With Bryan."

I resist the obvious retort. *That was so last week. Don't you read the paper?* But it's not her fault that she revolves in a different orbit than we do. "So why aren't you making her go to school?" I ask.

"She said she'd be home by ten." That's when I notice the sign blinking on Mom's forehead: NOT UP FOR DISCUSSION.

"Well, good night," I say.

"Good night, sleep tight, don't let the alligators bite."

I go back to my room. Bouncing on my mattress helps to settle me down. My sister likes a girl. Like likes. True, she lied to me all this time. But the new-and-improved Roz understands why. I haven't always been on her side lately. But I've matured since last summer. I'm finally the type of girl who can keep a secret or two. More or less. I know how to be a good friend. I still don't have the best taste in boys, but two out of three beats zero out of three. And I forgive her because:

She trusts me now. FINALLY.

She asked for my help.

She called me Slim.

Besides, I relish the romantic assignment to reunite star-crossed lovers. It's like courting Eva's ex-boyfriends, only better because I like Carmen more. Romantic frippery is one of my strong suits. In the end the princesses will live happily ever after in the castle. Of course, I'll have to slay a certain very short dragon first.

Unfortunately, I fall asleep before Eva returns home from "Bryan's house."

Wednesday morning, Eva comes into the kitchen dressed for school, and my excitement jumps upward to Level Orange. Sadly, I can't ask her a single question about last night because Mom happens to be in the kitchen with us. And really I should wait until Eva volunteers the information herself. Then a miracle happens when Mom offers to drive us.

"Roz and I are walking to school together," Eva says, heading out the door. Her girly-girl broomstick skirt and tunic top shimmer like jewels in the outside light. I scoop up her hand and walk with her in silence. It's so hard to keep quiet, I feel like Hercules on one of his tasks for the gods.

"Marshmallow got your tongue?" she says after torturing me for two blocks by not speaking. "You're curiously uncurious."

"I was trying to be the new Roz. But now that you've introduced the topic . . . when did you know?how did you know?who was your first crush?have you ever kissed a girl?what else do you do?what do you call yourself?bi or lesbian?who else knows?are you planning on telling the parents?did Bryan suspect?what really happened between you and Andie?did you know that over a thousand species of animals practice homosexuality . . . ?"

"Enough!" she says quickly. "That's too many questions, Slim."

I revel in the new nickname even though I came up with it myself. "Tell me what you want to," I say.

"Okay, I'll tell you something. But it doesn't answer a single one of your questions. It's about when you found the tampons in my room."

I slip on a wet patch, and she tightens her hand to steady me.

"I really did lie to make you feel better," she says, "but there's more to it." *Pregnant pause.* "Mom made such a big deal out of me getting my period. *You're a real woman now.* But I hadn't mastered being a girl yet. I wanted to postpone the whole thing. I already knew I was different from other girls."

I drape my arm over her shoulder. "We're all different. In some way or another. Take me."

"That's true. Still, you're pretty great . . . most of the time." Her grin says she's (mostly) teasing.

"You'll be calling me better than great when you've heard all the details of Operation Seduce Carmen."

Eva groans. "You're scaring me."

"Does Carmen know you like her?"

"Yes." Our shoes crunch on cold gravel as we cut through the park.

"Like like?"

"I'm guessing so." Eva picks up the pace then, and I'm forced to drop my arm from her shoulder. "I kissed her. The day before our fight at tryouts."

She's a little ahead of me now, so I can't see her face.

"Any tongue?" I ask. Tact will elude me my entire life no matter how tirelessly I pursue it. Admittedly I'm not trying that hard at the moment.

Eva turns around and swats me with her bag. "It freaked us both out, I think."

"Did it feel weird?"

"It felt . . . right. That's all I'm going to say about it. Now tell me about your covert operation."

"Step one," I say. "Nostalgia. Do something to remind her of one of your P. Tom escapades."

Eva stops walking and looks at me. Her face is flushed. "Carmen told you?"

"I found out. She carries the wrappers with her everywhere. That's a good sign."

Eva relaxes a little. "What else?"

"We can work on it tonight after rehearsal. So who was your first crush?" I ask.

No answer. I decide not to take her reticence personally.

We have all the time in the world to discuss details. Still, silence was invented for me to fill with chatter. "I remember mine," I say. "Jake French with the chin dimple. I probably told you about him a dozen times."

"Alyssa Todd," she says at last. "The girl who wore horseback-riding clothes all the time."

We're a block from school now, and since I don't want this conversation to ever end, I shorten my steps considerably. "I remember her. She had enormous hair."

Eva shifts her bag to the other side. "I used to daydream about braiding it."

"But you wrote stink about her in your di—" I stop myself almost in time.

Flight attendant: Miss, you're allowed only one carry-on.
Me: This is my carry-on. This other bag is for my big mouth.

Eva's expression reads smug. "That's because you read my decoy diary. *Today I woke up and brushed my teeth. Then I got dressed and went to school. Ran into Shay from Spanish class.* Sound familiar?"

I'm not the only Peterson with a touch of the serpent. "So what happened?" I ask.

"Nothing. I kissed Alyssa's brother in the shed one time."

"So you really do like boys?"

Despite my ever-shrinking step length, we've arrived at school. She stops walking, and I'm grateful. "All that stuff you said about dashboards and falling in love with whomever?" she says.

"Yeah?" BlueDragon runs over to greet us like we were lost for weeks in the Arctic tundra.

"Dead on. I'm so mad you figured it out first."

Eva loves me despite my big mouth and spying ways. Bliss. Even the fresh muddy paw prints on my pants don't upset me.

The obstacle to all my romantic schemes towers under me. She points toward the freezer. "Bring out five trays of lasagna," she says. I steal glances at her while I work. There's less than a zero percent chance she doesn't know about Carmen's orientation. She *is* omniscient after all.

"What do you think of Jonathan?" I ask as I whisk past her.

"I don't."

"You don't what?" I say, dropping a tray of lasagna on the counter next to the ovens. "Approve of him as boyfriend material?"

Felicia snorts. "He's not her boyfriend."

So the whole decoy boyfriend scheme failed. I think up a way to keep her talking without showing my hand, searching for a daisy to shield my next question.

"He's not her boyfriend now. But you wouldn't disown her if he was, would you?"

She narrows her eyes in a way that says shooting flames are in my future. I back up a few feet.

"I would never disown her. But I might ground her till her wedding day."

I scurry off to fetch another load from the freezer. Felicia won't allow poor Carmen a boyfriend, let alone a girlfriend.

When I deliver the next batch, she hands me a nail file.

"What's this for?" I ask. I imagine some new ordeal, an

enormous kitchen device that can only be cleaned with the tiny scraper at the end.

"For your nose."

My hand jumps upward.

"File it down so you can't poke it where it doesn't belong." She laughs. I laugh too, although more from nervousness than enjoyment. "Stop bothering me now." She sends me off with one of her patented slasher-movie smiles.

During a break in rehearsal, I drag Jonathan to the bathroom for some privacy and lean against the door so no one else can enter. "Eva could waste away from unrequited love."

"You're talking about Carmen?"

I knew he knew. Everyone knew. Except me. "Help me get them together," I say.

"You make the dinner reservation, and I'll play the violin for them."

"You play violin? I didn't know that."

"There's a lot you don't know." He rinses his hands at the sink and twirls the paper towel handle. I laugh. He doesn't know everything either, like that the dispenser has been empty since the Clinton administration.

"They'll have to keep their love a secret from Felicia."

"Tough assignment, Pixie." He dries his hands on my shirtsleeves.

I still have her nail file in my pocket to remind me of this fact. But should Carmen ruin her life to please her mom? Still, I'm wise enough to change the subject, a sore topic of conversation for Jonathan, given how his parents are behaving.

"After Touchstone, what next?" I say. "Macbeth? Hamlet?"

"I don't want no whitey role." He does the cool-black-dude hand thing.

"But you're half white."

"I'm black. See?" He shakes his Afro at me.

"That's denying half of yourself." The handle turns. I lean against the door with all my weight. "We're talking in here," I shout.

"It's like this," he says patiently. "If you're bisexual, are you half heterosexual? No way." The intruder pounds relentlessly. "You're a homo."

"Who are you calling a homo?" I ask, though he does have a point. The door cracks open an inch despite my best effort. Three bodies come flying in. "Office hours are over," I say.

"Do you mind staying after?" I ask Carmen when we finish the last scene of the day. "I want to go over my notes with you." I flatter her unmercifully for several minutes to put her in the best mood possible. After that, I take the plunge. "Eva asked me to give you this."

Carmen's eyes widen when she sees the pink envelope and bouquet of flowers. Her bottom lip trembles.

"And I have a little gift for you, too," I say. "You can play Rosalind on our second weekend. I'll do Phebe instead."

She sucks her lips inside her mouth. "Rich gifts wax poor when givers prove unkind," she says. Translation? She mistakes the nature of my devious machinations, having no idea to what lengths I will go for Eva's sake.

"I'm keeping the opening weekend for myself," I say.

She wrinkles her nose. "Why would you share the lead with me at all?"

"You're my friend, remember?"

While she's still dazed and confused by this bizarre turn of events, I drop a final hint.

"Promise me you'll call Eva."

She hides her face in her hands then. "I don't know if I can," she wails into her palms.

I meant to bring up Felicia, ask Carmen how much she knows and about her views on sexuality. But the scene has not unfolded like I planned it. I stuff the nail file deeper into my pocket.

The long day before opening night has arrived. AT LAST. The sun is barely up, and already I'm busy plotting details. There are bumper stickers to print, items to buy, and secrets to spill, all before homeroom. When I go to the kitchen for breakfast, Mom looks me up and down.

"Save your strength for the play," she says.

"I am."

She slops yogurt into the blender and sprinkles it with oat bran, protein powder, and flax seed. "Revenge is only skin deep," she says. She must be an FBI agent by night. Otherwise how would she know?

"What are you talking about?" I say.

"Your aura. It reminds me of the day you trashed Mrs. Halsinger's yard." The grind of the blender drowns out my protest.

Mrs. Hell-stinger can best be summarized as the Living Dead masquerading as a fourth-grade teacher. My mantra that year was Reduce, Reuse, and Recycle, but

Mrs. Hell-stinger wouldn't accept any homework on previously used paper. So I dumped a wheelbarrow full of garbage on her lawn and planted a sign on the summit that read OUR FUTURE WITHOUT THE THREE R'S.

Blender off.

"She wouldn't—" I attempt to say.

Blender on.

I politely drink the smoothie, despite the abundance of particulates at the bottom. Mom offers me seconds, which I refuse, making choking noises and begging for water. There are limits to good manners. When Mom unplugs the blender, I seize my chance.

"You're right," I say when I'm halfway out the door. "But sometimes you have to squeeze a few lemons to get lemonade."

Mom laughs.

I slap a new bumper sticker onto the DykeByke that reads 90% HETEROSEXUAL, 10% LESBIAN. I printed others with every split imaginable. I plan to leave them around campus for anyone to use as they wish.

At the pharmacy I bury a packet of condoms under a bottle of bath oil and a loofah pad in my basket. Unfortunately, the cashier remembers me from years ago when she worked as a librarian. Her lips go mighty thin as she rings me up. Zip-Stop Jenny gives me a different strange look when I empty her rack of Juicy Fruit gum. "It's for a joke," I say.

Chapter 25

In homeroom Mr. Beltz puts everyone to sleep with his unique brand of hypnosis, the Drone™. Except for us theater geeks. We are wound so tight we would spin like tops if we were set free. I shift in my chair for the zillionth time. Andie's bright orange eyeliner stands out against her pale skin, and her black pigtails have new yellow tips. My zebra nail polish fails to measure up. When will I ever learn? She lifts her notebook to half cover her face and whispers to me.

Her: You promised to do anything I asked.

Though I can barely hear her, the message comes through loud and clear. What now?

Me (raising a textbook to hide my lips): Uh-oh.
Her: I'm calling in your promise.
Me: And . . . ?
Her: I'll tell you tonight.

As long as she's my friend, I'll never be safe.

Her: Coming to lunch?

The lunch minute at the Barn before opening night is a theater-geek freak-out fest of major proportions. I hate to miss it.

Me: I can't.

Mr. Beltz drops an atlas onto his desk from such a height that the whack-noise startles me into silence. He is looking right at me. "I have an announcement," he says.

He can't flunk me out of homeroom, but he can send me to detention.

"I'm so sorry for talking, Mr. Beltz. It was very rude of me. I'll try to do better," I blurt out in a futile attempt to save myself.

He laughs aloud—an unfamiliar occurrence—and the sound that comes out of his mouth is more girlish giggle than guyish guffaw. I like him better already. The next thing he says, though, astounds me.

"I have an announcement," he repeats. "Our very own Rosella Peterson will star in *As You Like It* tonight at seven thirty P.M. You can buy tickets for the performance at the main office. I already bought mine. For both Friday and Saturday night. I'm looking forward to it, Roz. Break a leg."

"I will," I say. "Uh . . . I don't mean I'll break a leg, of course. I mean thank you. See you tonight. Well, I might not see you exactly. You'll see me, though," I say. Who can blame me for blathering? It's the shock.

". . . Sprain an ankle . . . omigod . . . my boobs can't breathe in this . . . your eyelashes are coming unglued . . . this gel is useless . . . he said what? . . . I'd rather do it in the backseat than . . ." I love the chaos backstage on opening night. Twenty minutes till curtain, and I'm walk-on ready. I hide behind a backdrop near where my parents are seated in the front row. Mr. Beltz takes a seat next to them and starts a conversation. Judging from their happy faces, it appears he isn't informing them about my propensity to communicate overmuch in class.

After scanning the audience for Felicia (I see neither claw nor fang of her), I return to the backstage zone. Eyeliner Andie and Jonathan are AWOL, and the level of panic rises by the minute. Carmen—a cell phone attached to her ear like a giant silver tick—stands at the edge of the Mosh Pit calling every number she knows, which includes half of Yolo Bluffs. I tug at her sleeve to get her attention.

"They'll be here," I say.

Eva beckons me to a quiet spot. "Give me audience, good madam," she says.

"Is this about Operation Seduce Carmen?" I ask.

"Shut up. I P-Tommed her window last night, but she didn't wake up. And she's preoccupied at the moment, so I haven't gotten to talk to her. Where's the bouquet?"

"Behind the speaker."

"Thanks, Slim," she says. She straightens the sleeve of my dress and untangles a strand of my long wig hair. "I'll answer another one of your questions from the other day now."

"Which one?"

"About Andie. I kissed her once last year . . . as an experiment. It didn't work out. For her, either." She has a teasing glint in her eye. "So who are you setting your sights on at the cast party tonight? Andie? Nico? Bryan? All three?"

"I'm not that greedy."

"Boy or girl?"

"Hermaphrodite," I say. "What about you?"

"I'm not the rebel you are, but I'll go for what I want."

"Someone has to fight the fight," I say.

"And you're the person for the job."

"The more pity, that fools may not speak wisely what wise men do foolishly," I say. Translation? She's so smart, I wish we were sisters. Oh. That's right. We are.

She pulls me into a hug, a syrupy Hallmark moment, to be sure. I enjoy it.

"I thank thee for your love to me," she says, "which thou shalt find I will most kindly requite."

A screech from the Mosh Pit rudely interrupts our tender exchange. "I'm going to kill you now!" Carmen has Andie by the shoulders.

"Be gentle," Andie says. "This outfit took me hours to put together." The tresses on the left side of her fuchsia wig are twice as long as those on the right. Her costume has suffered other alterations, shredded tulle sleeves, a thick black silk choker, thigh-high boots, and a large metal buckle across her skirt. She looks stunning. "Before you say anything, you have to see Jonathan."

The theater lights blink. Jonathan appears striding toward us in black leather boots accented with chains. A buckle to match Andie's adorns the lapel of his long trench coat. They make a cute neo-Goth-punk couple.

I'm indignant, of course. "Why were you so secretive?" I say. "We could've updated all the costumes. We could've renamed the play *Whichever Way You Like It: A Tale of Confused Goth Love*. I own the perfect dress."

Jonathan wraps his arm around my waist and gives me

a reassuring squeeze that says we're friends forever. "Sally," he says.

"What?" I ask.

"What, what?" He flashes me a mischievous smile. "Sally is Sapphire's real name."

When the lights go down, Bryan and his servant make their entrance. Silence reigns backstage because every noise except the faintest of whispers carries forward. Eva and I will go on next. I feel myself slip into character, the witty young daughter of the banished king on the brink of falling in love.

In the scrape of props between scenes, I overhear Jonathan ask Carmen, "Is your mom coming?"

"I don't think so," Carmen says.

Wax-hearted lockbox! I invent a new Elizabethan curse on the spot. We'll pry her open and melt that waxy heart yet. Carmen sees me eavesdropping and waves me onto the stage.

"I pray thee, Rosalind, sweet my coz, be merry," Eva says to me.

In an instant, I become the sad-eyed and wise Rosalind. After some banter, we make our way to the palace to watch Bryan's wrestling match. He throws down Charles, and I call him over to give him a token of my esteem.

"Gentleman, wear this for me," I say. But instead of handing him a necklace, I lay two condoms across his palm. Out of their wrappers. Eva's superior skill keeps her from breaking character. Poor Bryan, though, flushes under his makeup and stumbles over his next line.

Eva and I exit before the end of the scene.

"What was that about?" she mouths.

"What?" I mouth back. And then we're onstage again.

At intermission Bryan drags me out the side door and pins me against the wall. Think Tom Cruise in *Top Gun*.

"Thanks for the gift," he says, staring at my mouth. Slowly, slowly he moves in toward me until his lips brush against mine. The kiss feels good. He pulls back for a moment and serenades me. "The horn, the horn, the lusty horn, is not a thing to laugh to scorn." Or is he serenading his boner?

In the midst of all the buzzing and tingling, I make my final decision. I want to be with someone I love and who loves me. Bryan loves only himself. I shove him away.

"*Dankish puttock,*" I say, in case he doesn't get my meaning.

"You gave me two condoms in front of a hundred people," he says.

"I bought them for your girlfriends," I say. "Those freshman girls you've been making out with, Bunny and Bimbo. I believe in safe sex." Thus ends my obsession with Wenching Boy. I abandon him there, his face a mask of disbelief.

The audience quiets down for the final two acts, a whirlwind of wooing and double-edged exchanges. Carmen pushes BlueDragon onto the stage for the scene where a wild lioness attacks Orlando. BlueDragon barks twice and shakes his fake mane before leaping into the laps of those in the front row—a stylish exit, to be sure. He earns the biggest laugh of the show.

"There you are," Andie says when I'm offstage watching from the wings. She cups a hand over my ear. "So here's the deal about your promise. If Nico kisses you, you have to kiss him back."

"But he's your boyfriend," I say rather too loudly. A stage tech stares at me. Hopefully the entire audience didn't hear.

"That was temporary. I thought that since you only want what you can't have—"

"You snake."

"If you mean I'm clever, I accept the compliment."

"You don't want him?"

"I like you both. Like like. Together," she says sweetly. "Loose now and then a scatter'd smile, and that I'll live upon." Translation? Andie invented a category for herself that the famous sexologist Alfred Kinsey never dreamed of. She's a no-sexual attracted to a couple. "You can invite me on a few of your dates," she adds.

Near the end of the play, I corner Nico by the Mosh Pit. If he's going to kiss me tonight, I want to know something first.

"What do you like about me?" I ask him, reverting to my patented nonsubtle approach. A bull in a china shop sounds so old-fashioned. Think a herd of goats in a clothing boutique. His hair hides his eyes as usual. Fortunately, I know the bottom half of his face rather well by now, especially his mouth. I imagine his lips on my lips. He ate fake dog doo, and I ate a banana slug. We're made for each other.

"You don't get scared by things," he says to me. "You go for what you want."

That sets my heart aflutter. Love looks not with the eyes, but with the mind, and therefore is wing'd Cupid painted blind. Translation? Through all that hair, Nico has caught a glimpse of the real me. I want him to kiss me this second. Unfortunately, telekinesis is not my strong suit. We stand close together like trees in the forest until I'm called back onstage.

In the final act, I throw off my manly garb and marry Bryan. The other players are paired off and married, not as expected, but more or less happily. I perform the epilogue and the curtain falls to applause. When the curtain rises again, the minor actors run forward, bow, and move aside to make room for the stars. We hold hands as couples—Bryan and I at the center. Eva and Noah, Nico and Carmen, and Andie and Jonathan stand on either side of us.

The audience keeps up the clap and stomp. We bow a second time. Then Bryan puts his arm around the small of my back, tips me over, and kisses me. The crowd goes wild. When the curtain comes down, Nico charges us, knocking Bryan and me over so we sprawl to the boards. Bryan scrambles to his feet.

"So graceful," I say.

When the curtain rises Nico is kneeling over me. The audience explodes with surprised laughter. "I am he that is so love shaked," he says to me in a voice loud enough for all to hear. "I pray you, tell me your remedy."

"Then come kiss me, sweet and twenty," I reply. Telekinesis may not be my strong suit. Improvisation is. I wrap my arms around his neck and pull him toward me. It turns out that he's an excellent kisser. The curtain falls and rises a third time, and we're still kissing. Some things are more important than who buys your underwear.

After the final curtain rises, I thrust a bouquet of yellow roses into Carmen's arms. Jonathan piles a second bouquet on top of mine, and Andie a third. While she stands buried in flowers, Eva adds a stranger bouquet to the company, one made with skewers topped with packets of Juicy Fruit. Carmen flushes and hugs her. My parents rush the stage.

"They make a darling couple, don't they?" Mom says to me. She's smiling at Eva and Carmen. Dad winks. Am I detecting a startling absence of cluelessness? Love is thicker than water, after all.

When the proud parents finally leave the stage, we geeks troop to the Mosh Pit to decompress. A shout cuts through the celebratory wildness. "What the . . . ?" It sounds like Bryan's voice, but I can't see him in the crowd.

The chaos in the Mosh Pit comes to a rubber-burning halt. Someone screams.

"What's happening?" Carmen shouts.

A small explosion rips through the air. For one sick second, I remember the alien assassin who threatened my life. Then I catch sight of Bryan's freshman girlfriend holding a strange weapon. She's pointing it at Bryan. Blue paint drips down his front from his chin to navel. The tabloid headline reads TWO-TIMING BASTARD GETS HIS JUST DESSERTS—PAINT BALL SUNDAE. When I showed Bunny the photos of Bryan kissing Bimbo, I had no idea she would take revenge like this. Honest.

As Shakespeare says (with liberties), "It is not my way to beg, so I will not beg you to love this story. But to the people who care, I charge you to like as much of this story as please you. And for the rest, take it As You Like It." Translation? Love me for who I am or not at all. I'll do my best to be worthy.

Epilogue

Three amazing things happened in the weeks following opening night. Nico and I became a couple. We go well together, and I discovered what it's like to do something without considering my audience. To do something just for me. To be honest, I'm a tad embarrassed to be seen smooching with him in public, but that will pass. In the end you have to pick who you are (there are so many choices!) and go with it.

Felicia came to watch Carmen play Rosalind on the second weekend. Carmen performed magnificently, btw. After the show ended, she let her mother hug her in front of everyone. For a few seconds, I thought Felicia might go misty-eyed. In the end she didn't, but she came dangerously close to shedding a tear or two.

The best bit is the last bit. Eva and I are real sisters again. My streak of breaking glassware—butterflies, vases, umbrella stands, car windows, and such—ended just like Sierra predicted it would. And though Eva is not yet ready to come out in Yolo Bluffs, she asked for MY help posting her coming-out story online. Good thing she did because a few parts needed editing.

I'm a senior in high school and a very private person. Let me rephrase that. Extremely private. I had my first crush on a girl in the fourth grade. My shyness kept me from admitting it. Even to myself. There was no need to because I liked boys too. A lot. When I understood the truth about myself a few years later, I wanted to confide in my little sister. But she didn't want me to be anything but perfect. And I worried (wrongly!) that she would tell everyone.

A few months ago, I realized I was in love with my best friend. But I didn't do anything about it. Until one day I kissed her. When she told me she felt the same, I panicked and left. The next day she invented an excuse to end our friendship. I was miserable. So miserable I decided to risk asking my sister for help. And she got us together again (but that's another story). I'm so lucky that Roz is my sister.

Lexicon of Shakespearean Insults

Beef-witted—with the wits of a dead cow.

Beslubbering—like slobbering only worse.

Boil-brained—with lesions on your brain that make you stupid.

Canker-blossom—a person like an open sore that pretends to be a flower.

Clack-dish—someone whose prattle transcends mere loquaciousness.

Clotpole—blockhead. It sounds much worse than blockhead, I know.

Coxcomb—a boy who thinks he's cuter than he actually is. That's the type I tend to fall for.

Craven—cowardly in a most contemptible way.

Dankish—suffering from a coat of mold and mildew.

Dissembling—lying, cheating, and hypocritical.

Dog-hearted—cruel, inhuman. This in no way refers to BlueDragon's loving heart.

Eye-offending—get-out-of-my-sight ugly.

Fen-sucked—sucked out from a marsh. I'm not joking.

Flap-mouthed—verbose, as in talkative (like me).

Flax-wench—a prostitute.

Flirt-gill—an empty-headed person who thinks every boy on the planet belongs to her.

Fly-bitten—bitten by flies, you clotpole (see Clotpole).

Folly-fallen—victimized by one's own evil schemes.

Foot-licker—a suck-up of major proportions.

Gorbellied—more than just round in the middle.

Harpy—a ravenous and filthy bird with a woman's head and a bird's body. Ouch!

Hedge-born—a person born under a hedge. Really.

Horn-beast—a devil, and I don't mean the sexy kind.

Knavish—ill-behaved and unprincipled. An adjective you don't want in front of your name.

Malignancy—a hideous and incurable disease.

Measle—an open sore filled with pus.

Mewling—whiny in the worst way.

Moldwarp—a mole.

Plume-plucked—stripped of one's lovely feathers.

Puttock—a marshy, mud-besmirched sort of person. Smelly, too.

Rabbit-sucker—a weasel, and I don't mean the cute, furry kind.

Rampallion—something worse than a rapscallion.

Ratsbane—the trioxide of arsenic. For the chemistry impaired, that means poison.

Scullion—a kitchen slave.

Sheep-biting—more annoying than a horsefly.

Simp—a simple person, and I don't mean uncomplicated. More like simpleminded.

Sour-faced—you get like this if you spend too much time sucking on lemons.

Swag-bellied—paunchy.

Unchin-snouted—with a nose like an unchin. What's an unchin you ask? Who knows?

Wenching—a wormy behavior that involves stringing several girls along at once.

Whey-faced—pale from fear.

Acknowledgments

Writing is a solitary occupation. Still, you need a roomful of people to make an actual book. And I'm like a VW bug with an unreliable motor. It takes a lot of TLC to keep me running.

Thank you, Pelle, Drake, and Leif for all your love, encouragement, and patience. Thank you, Dad, for giving me days off from school to write when I was little. Thank you, Deborah Schweninger, for saying, "You wrote a real novel!" Your belief in me fills my gas tank.

Many others have given me a push-start along the way: Jennifer Badger, Elana Lombard, Ana-Ruth Aldana, Hilary Cushing-Murray, John Nichols, Jessica Gormley, Beth Enson, Elsbeth Atencio, Margaret Badger, Madeleine Herrmann, Joseph Hardegree, and Steve Deitsch. Thank you all. And thank you to those I didn't mention by name.

I'm grateful to A.J. Usherwood, Nancy Jenkins, and the Taos High drama students for inviting me to rehearsals of *A Midsummer's Night Rave.*

Without my incomparable critique partners—Kimber MacDonald, Jean-Marie Jackson, Miriam Goin, Ellie Crowe, Todd Wynward, and Morgan Farley—I'd still be in the parking lot.

Thank you, Monika Bjorkman, for giving me your birthday wishes.

Hats off to Stephen Fraser for your insightful editorial suggestions when I lost my way.

Cheers and champagne to the hard-working people at Inkwell and Henry Holt, but especially my agent, Catherine Drayton, and my editor, Kate Farrell. And to Robert Boswell for making the introduction.

Hugs to my sister, Jolene Welch, for remaining my friend through thick and thin.